Fortune Hunters

Author: Jack Cull
Developer: Matt Finch
Editor: Jeff Harkness
5e Conversion: Edwin Nagy
Art Direction: Casey Christofferson
Layout and Graphic Design: Charles A. Wright
Cover Design: Suzy Moseby
Cover Art: Colin Chan
Interior Art: Brett Blakely, Thuan Pham, Sid Quade, Erica Willey

FROG GOD GAMES IS:

Bill Webb, Matthew J. Finch, Zach Glazar, Charles A. Wright, Edwin Nagy, Mike Badolato, John Barnhouse

FROG GOD GAMES

ISBN: 978-1-6656-0006-4

TABLE OF CONTENTS

INTRODUCTION

The wonderful thing about non-player characters is that they give life to a game. Interesting NPCs make a game feel unique and special, especially when players get to interact with them (for better or worse). Not only that, but they help the players feel like they are playing in a real world, and that their actions matter to people. And over time, these characters grow alongside the players, making the stakes of the adventure greater. A map and adventures are great, but the places need to be populated in order to make them feel alive.

The NPCs presented in this book are given three stats blocks: one each for challenge ratings of 3, 6, and 10. While each character has a description, these different stat blocks are also accompanied by informational text about the characters at that point in their life (what was going on with them at Challenge 3. How are they different now at Challenge 6? And even more so at Challenge 10). We did this to allow Gamemasters to have NPCs that could grow and advance along with the players. Perhaps an NPC is an early adversary for them, but they either get away, are allowed to live, or the players simply never engage them in combat to the death. The Gamemaster can now decide that enough time has gone by and use the next stat block iteration up (3 to 6, or 6 to 10) to allow for a greater challenge. And who knows, with what the NPCs go through behind the scenes, perhaps they eventually become an ally. Or maybe an ally character becomes an enemy!

We decided to do the characters this way so that you, the Gamemaster, have the tools to create a living, breathing world your players can interact with as it evolves through time. While it doesn't have to be done for every character, we wanted the NPCs here to help bring Cat's Cradle to life, to help the players connect with the people and places they come across. Gamemasters are welcome to add onto the stories presented, omit what they don't like, or tie something in directly to their adventure or campaign to make everything feel even more connected. Whether they be allies to fight alongside, antagonists to stop, shopkeepers to interact with, or simply quest-givers for the party, each character is unique and contributes to the overall roleplaying experience.

ARIVER KYDAM

This tall, sallow-skinned young human knight holds himself rigidly in his ill-fitting plate armor. His shoulder-length greasy black hair frames his gaunt, hawk-nosed face as he glares at the "plebs" that occupy the street around him. He rests his gauntleted hand on the hilt of his longsword, waiting for an excuse to draw his blade and declare a duel against anyone who dares challenges him.

The third son of a local noble family, Ariver Kydam was born with a silver spoon in his mouth, and he loves to pull his noble birth rank whenever he can, typically demanding either first refusals or preferential treatment. Flanking him at all times are a few of his friends that he uses as backup when he hopes to intimidate those that get in his way or have something he wants. His stuck-up arrogance is known the instant words come out of his mouth, usually in the form of an insult or snide comment. In addition, Ariver can often be found observing the scene of a crime being investigated by the local guards, although it is never from the standpoint of having any sympathy for the victim(s). Instead he enjoys seeing the aftermath of the risky and dangerous lifestyle that criminals lead, and while he would never socialize with them openly, wishes to have a connection with the criminal underworld.

ARIVER KYDAM

Medium humanoid, lawful evil

Armor Class 14 (chain shirt)
Hit Points 52 (8d8 +16)
Speed 30 ft.

STR	DEX	CON	INT	WIS	CHA
16 (+3)	13 (+1)	14 (+2)	12 (+1)	10 (+0)	15 (+2)

Saving Throws Con +4, Cha +4
Skills Insight +2, Intimidation +4
Senses passive Perception 10
Languages Common, Elvish
Challenge 3 (700 XP)

Reckless. At the start of his turn, Ariver can gain advantage on all melee weapon attack rolls he makes during that turn, but attack rolls against him have advantage until the start of his next turn.

***Reinforcements* (1/day).** Once per day, Ariver may call upon 1d4 + 1 of his friends to assist him in any situation. Treat these as **nobles**. This ability does not work if Ariver is unable to speak.

Actions

Multiattack. Ariver makes two melee attacks.

Longsword. *Melee Weapon Attack:* +5 to hit, reach 5 ft., one target. *Hit:* 7 (1d8 + 3) slashing damage, or 8 (1d10 + 3) slashing damage if used with two hands.

Longbow. *Ranged Weapon Attack:* +3 to hit, range 150/600 ft., one target. *Hit:* 5 (1d8 + 1) piercing damage

Reactions

Parry. Ariver adds 2 to his AC against one melee attack that would hit him. To do so, he must see the attacker and be wielding a melee weapon.

Humiliated from a previous encounter with a group of do-gooders, Ser Kydam began looking for an extra edge in combat, more than simply his childhood friends to support him in battle. Not only has he improved his overall combat prowess, but Ariver has greased the palms of some local guardsmen to "shake down" his adversaries prior to any physical engagement. In addition, he has been able to use his increasing noble status to be the legitimate front for the shady dealings of a smuggling-focused thieves' guild known as the "Wharf Rats" that deals out of Old Town and the Docks. Because of this, Ariver can call upon a half dozen rogue thugs that shadow him throughout town to join in any conflict he engages in. He does not ever join in any of the smuggling or thieving enterprises but is always hungry to hear of the nitty gritty details once the venture has been completed.

ARIVER KYDAM

Medium humanoid, lawful evil

Armor Class 16 (half plate)
Hit Points 78 (12d8 + 24)
Speed 30 ft.

STR	DEX	CON	INT	WIS	CHA
17 (+3)	14 (+2)	15 (+2)	13 (+1)	10 (+0)	15 (+2)

Saving Throws Con +5, Cha +5
Skills Insight +3, Intimidation +5
Senses passive Perception 10
Languages Common, Elvish
Challenge 6 (2,300 XP)

Reckless. At the start of his turn, Ariver can gain advantage on all melee weapon attack rolls he makes during that turn, but attack rolls against him have advantage until the start of his next turn.

Reinforcements (1/day). Ariver may call upon 1d6 + 2 corrupt city guards to assist him in any situation. Treat the guards as **thugs.** This ability does not work if Ariver is unable speak.

Sneak Attack (1/turn). Ariver deals an extra 7 (2d6) damage when he hits a target with a weapon attack and has advantage on the attack roll, or when the target is within 5 feet of an ally his that isn't incapacitated and Ariver doesn't have disadvantage on the attack roll.

Actions

Multiattack. Ariver makes two melee attacks or two ranged attacks.

Longsword. *Melee Weapon Attack:* +6 to hit, reach 5 ft., one target. *Hit:* 7 (1d8 + 3) slashing damage, or 8 (1d10 + 3) slashing damage if used with two hands.

Longbow. *Ranged Weapon Attack:* +5 to hit, range 150/600 ft., one target. *Hit:* 6 (1d8 + 2) piercing damage

Reactions

Parry. Ariver adds 3 to his AC against one melee attack that would hit him. To do so, he must see the attacker and be wielding a melee weapon.

Ariver Kydam has become a noble of the court under Baron Scale within Cat's Cradle and the area around it, having a small keep in a province a few miles from the city proper. He has amassed a great deal of wealth from his criminal connections, and due to the fact that he had his two older brothers assassinated, he acquired his inherited position when his parents died. Since his severe scarring and disfigurement from a previous fight with troublesome "good" adversaries, Ariver has become a bitter, jealous, and short-fused man, Lord Kydam primarily stays in his keep, but commands a small military force that patrols his lands and enforces his iron-fisted rule. His criminal connections have also expanded: not only have the Wharf Rats smuggling organization grown in their enterprise in the city, but Ariver has known ties with the Crimson Skull pirates, the Crystal Husk witch coven from deep within the Forest of Cantricle, and even the Black Tongue assassins that work out of the city of Voles to the North.

ARIVER KYDAM

Medium humanoid, lawful evil

Armor Class 18 (plate)
Hit Points 120 (16d8 + 48)
Speed 30 ft.

STR	DEX	CON	INT	WIS	CHA
18 (+4)	15 (+2)	16 (+3)	14 (+3)	11 (+0)	15 (+2)

Saving Throws Con +7, Cha +6
Skills Insight +4, Intimidation +6
Senses passive Perception 10
Languages Common, Elvish
Challenge 10 (5,900 XP)

Reckless. At the start of his turn, Ariver can gain advantage on all melee weapon attack rolls he makes during that turn, but attack rolls against him have advantage until the start of his next turn.

Reinforcements (1/day). Ariver may call upon 2d6 members of the criminal underworld to assist him in any situation. Treat these criminals as **bandit captains.** This ability does not work if Ariver is unable speak.

Sneak Attack (1/turn). Ariver deals an extra 10 (3d6) damage when he hits a target with a weapon attack and has advantage on the attack roll, or when the target is within 5 feet of an ally his that isn't incapacitated and Ariver doesn't have disadvantage on the attack roll.

Well Connected. Ariver can use his influence to get himself out of any unfavorable criminal, political, or social enterprise he may or may not be caught being involved in. It is up to your discretion as to how many times this ability can be used, and its overall extent.

Actions

Multiattack. Ariver makes three melee attacks or two ranged attacks.

Longsword. *Melee Weapon Attack:* +8 to hit, reach 5 ft., one target. *Hit:* 8 (1d8 + 4) slashing damage, 9 (1d10 + 4) slashing damage if used with two hands.

Longbow. *Ranged Weapon Attack:* +6 to hit, range 150/600 ft., one target. *Hit:* 6 (1d8 + 2) piercing damage

Reactions

Parry. Ariver adds 4 to his AC against one melee attack that would hit him. To do so, he must see the attacker and be wielding a melee weapon.

AULRICH STEELSPADE

The brow of the dark skinned dwarven proprietor cannot help but furrow as he observes the crowd of individuals that occupy his establishment. The owner of the The Rebellious Boggart Tavern and Game Hall stands confidently with his hands firmly on the second-floor railing as he stares over it onto the ground floor below. Both his slicked back black hair and long braided bandholz beard are groomed perfectly, matching his freshly laundered and pressed nobleman attire, perfectly tailored to fit his wide muscular frame. The glint of a mithril chain shirt can be spotted from his open shirt, and while a scimitar is strapped to his belt, a warhammer leans within arm's reach.

Aulrich Steelspade is a gruff, foul-mouthed dwarf originally from the areas around the city of Voles to the North. He doesn't speak to anyone about the details of his youth, but it has been gathered over the years that he was on the run and hunted. Through the random anecdotes he grumbles off from time to time, many have theorized that it either included a mighty debt, a catastrophic fire, or a great number of people killed (perhaps even all three!). Whatever the case may be, Aulrich came to Cat's Cradle to start a new life for himself and found himself joining the late Baron in the Salt Wars. When the fighting was over, and with the connections and wealth he acquired, he decided to open a business in the budding town: The Rebellious Boggart Tavern and Game Hall, and business is good. And while he employs a variety of staff (from bartenders to wait staff, entertainers to croupiers, and even his own alchemist team hidden away in the cellar) Aulrich is always looking for trustworthy freelancers to check out the competition throughout town.

AULRICH STEELSPADE

Medium humanoid, lawful neutral

Armor Class 14 (chain shirt)
Hit Points 60 (8d8 + 24)
Speed 30 ft.

STR	DEX	CON	INT	WIS	CHA
16 (+3)	13 (+1)	17 (+3)	15 (+2)	14 (+2)	13 (+1)

Saving Throws Str +5, Cha +3
Skills Deception +3, Insight +6, Perception +4, Persuasion +5
Senses passive Perception 14
Languages Common, Dwarvish, Elvish, Goblin
Challenge 3 (700 XP)

Elusive Target. If Aulrich moves more than 5 feet on his turn, he adds 2 to his AC until the beginning of his next turn.
Stubborn and Resilient. Aulrich has advantage on saving throws against being charmed, frightened, or poisoned.

Actions

Multiattack. Aulrich makes two melee attacks.
Scimitar. *Melee Weapon Attack:* +5 to hit, reach 5 ft., one target. *Hit:* 6 (1d6 + 3) slashing damage.
Warhammer. *Melee Weapon Attack:* +5 to hit, reach 5 ft., one target. *Hit:* 7 (1d8 + 3) bludgeoning damage, or 8 (1d10+3) bludgeoning damage if used with two hands.

Aulrich finds himself in a bit of pickle these days. In his attempt to expand his ownership over various businesses throughout the city of Cat's Cradle, he has inadvertently upset a rival businessperson in town who has strong political ties to nobles in Baron Scale's circles, an elven entrepreneur by the name of Willowren Skystar. While there hasn't been any open conflict between Willowren and Aulrich, each has been sending agents to spy on and disrupt each other's interests in Cat's Cradle. He has reached out to some of the other tavern and inn owners in Old Town and the Gold District (such as the Upper Crust Inn and Treesa's Pub) in an attempt to gain support. As their establishments are streets apart from one another, and not in any direct competition with one another, Aulrich hopes to create an alliance that serves to be mutually beneficial for all involved, while also undermining the enterprises of Ser Skystar.

AULRICH STEELSPADE

Medium humanoid, lawful neutral

Armor Class 14 (chain shirt)
Hit Points 90 (12d8 + 36)
Speed 30 ft.

STR	DEX	CON	INT	WIS	CHA
16 (+3)	13 (+1)	17 (+3)	15 (+2)	15 (+2)	14 (+2)

Saving Throws Str +6, Cha +5
Skills Deception +5, Insight +8, Perception +5, Persuasion +8
Condition Immunities disease
Senses passive Perception 15
Languages Common, Dwarvish, Elvish, Goblin
Challenge 6 (2,300 XP)

Elusive Target. If Aulrich moves more than 5 feet on his turn, he adds 3 to his AC against until the beginning of his next turn.
Stubborn and Resilient. Aulrich has advantage on saving throws against being charmed, frightened, or poisoned.

Actions

Multiattack. Aulrich makes two melee attacks.
Scimitar. *Melee Weapon Attack:* +6 to hit, reach 5 ft., one target. *Hit:* 6 (1d6 + 3) slashing damage.
Warhammer. *Melee Weapon Attack:* +6 to hit, reach 5 ft., one target. *Hit:* 7 (1d8 + 3) bludgeoning damage, or 8 (1d10 + 3) bludgeoning damage if used with two hands.

Reactions

Strike Back. Aulrich may make a melee weapon attack against a creature that hits him with their own melee weapon attack. To do this, the attacker must be within reach and Aulrich must be able to see his attacker.

Having recently recovered from an assassination attempt on his life, Aulrich is even more gruff and rough in nature but is invigorated with a new level of determination and gusto for life. Unlike in years past, where the tavern owner would keep a reasonable distance from the general crowds that frequent his establishment, choosing to observe them from his private interior second story balcony that overlooks the entirety of the main floor hall of the tavern, he instead sits openly at a game table near the main bar. Aulrich is usually accompanied by one of his lieutenants and a scribe or courier to take and deliver notes, as well as an entertainer of some description. While he keeps his disdain for the current rulership in check to avoid any direct trouble with Baron Scale's men, Aulrich has begun secretly communicating with interested parties in the rival city of Five-and-Copper to the East.

AULRICH STEELSPADE

Medium humanoid, lawful neutral

Armor Class 14 (chain shirt)
Hit Points 120 (16d8 + 48)
Speed 30 ft.

STR	DEX	CON	INT	WIS	CHA
19 (+4)	14 (+2)	17 (+3)	15 (+2)	15 (+2)	15 (+2)

Saving Throws Str +8, Cha +6
Skills Deception +6, Insight +10, Perception +6, Persuasion +10
Condition Immunities charmed, disease, frightened, poison
Senses passive Insight 20, passive Perception 16
Languages Common, Dwarvish, Elvish, Goblin
Challenge 10 (5,900 XP)

Elusive Target. If Aulrich moves more than 5 feet on his turn, he adds 4 to his AC until the beginning of his next turn.
Stubborn Aura. Aulrich and any allies within 30 feet of him gain a +2 bonus to saving throws. Allies also have advantage on saving throws against being charmed or frightened. This ability is lost if Aulrich is incapacitated or unconscious.
Special Equipment. Aulrich wears *gauntlets of ogre power*. Without the gauntlets, his strength is 16.

Multiattack. Aulrich makes two melee attacks.
Scimitar. Melee Weapon Attack: +8 to hit, reach 5 ft., one target.
   Hit: 7 (1d6+4) slashing damage.
Warhammer. Melee Weapon Attack: +8 to hit, reach 5 ft., one
   target. *Hit:* 8 (1d8+4) bludgeoning damage, or 9 (1d10+4)
   bludgeoning damage if used with two hands.

Reactions

Strike Back. Aulrich may make a melee weapon attack against a
   creature that attacks with their own melee weapon, regardless
   if they succeeded in hitting him or not. To do this, the attacker
   must be within reach and Aulrich must be able to see his
   attacker.

Baron Scale

*A young and inexperienced baron, Scale is only nineteen years old. He is
an even-tempered and serious young man, friendly to everyone regardless of
status. While it is clear that most of the running of Cat's Cradle is being handled
by Scale's mother and advisers, it is also clear that Scale takes an interest in
every subject and takes seriously his duties and responsibilities. He listens to
all sides of a matter before approving his advisers' recommendations, seeking
to truly understand all sides of an issue before he signs off on their decisions.*

Because he is working hard to finish his education while participating fully
in his baronial duties, Scale is always busy. His advisers book those social
events they think will benefit his long term position as baron, and Scale makes
little other room in his schedule for relaxation or entertainment. Those seeking
an audience must either convince his advisers that a meeting is worthwhile,
wait through the long lines to address him publicly during his twice-a-week
all-comers audience hall, get invited to the sorts of parties he must attend
for networking purposes, or catch him during a rare quiet moment, such as
between his various daily lessons. This last is perhaps the most difficult, as his
guards rarely let strangers close.

BARON SCALE

Medium human, lawful good

Armor Class 17 (half plate)
Hit Points 77 (14d10)
Speed 30 ft.

STR	DEX	CON	INT	WIS	CHA
13 (+1)	15 (+2)	11 (+0)	15 (+2)	17 (+3)	18 (+4)

Saving Throws Int +4, Wis +5
Skills History +4, Insight +5, Intimidation +6, Persuasion +6
Senses passive Perception 13
Languages Common, Dwarvish
Challenge 3 (700 XP)

Well-guarded. Baron Scale is constantly accompanied by 2–8
   loyal bodyguards (**guards**).

Actions

Rapier. Melee Weapon Attack: +4 to hit, reach 5 ft., one target.
   Hit: 6 (1d8 + 2) piercing damage.

At the age of 27, Baron Scale is handsome, charming, and masterful,
easily able to take command of any situation. He is even-tempered and highly
energetic, but he keeps himself very busy, making little time for relaxation or
entertainment. That said, Scale does make time for networking events with the
city's wealthy and higher-class. In charm and bearing he can seem so perfect
at times that it is difficult to believe he is real, or that he is merely a baron.

Underneath this perfect veneer, however, Scale shows signs of a cunning
intellect and a shrewd skill for manipulation. Indeed, as courteous and charming
as he is, the man is also often difficult to read or predict. What is certain is that
Cat's Cradle is prospering under his rule, and his common people like and
respect him. The aristocracy and well-to-do seem to find Scale less flawless

— far too concerned for their tastes with the plight of the commoner — but so
charming and clever they can't quite seem to dislike him either.

Scale is known to possess a serviceable skill with his ancestors' renowned
enchanted blade, and to deal honestly with those who deal honestly with him.
Due to his strict instructions to his advisers, it is easiest to gain an audience
with him by using the right key phrases in requesting an appointment. Scale's
secretaries will make appointments for well-spoken, respectfully-garbed
visitors (regardless of social class) if they can make a good case for their visit
to the baron being beneficial to all the people of his holdings. Scale is said to
have no interest in his own personal gain, though — as he is quite a wealthy
man — this may be an exaggeration.

BARON SCALE

Medium human, lawful good

Armor Class 18 (*+1 half plate*)
Hit Points 99 (18d8 + 18)
Speed 30 ft., swim 30 ft.

STR	DEX	CON	INT	WIS	CHA
13 (+1)	15 (+2)	13 (+1)	16 (+3)	17 (+3)	18 (+4)

Saving Throws Int +6, Wis +6
Skills History +6, Insight +6, Intimidation +7, Performance
   (oratory) +7, Persuasion +7
Senses passive Perception 16
Languages Common, Dwarvish
Challenge 6 (2300 XP)

Well-guarded. Baron Scale is constantly accompanied by 2–8
   loyal bodyguards (**guards**).

Actions

Multiattack. The Baron makes two Ancestral Rapier attacks.
Ancestral Rapier (+2 flame tongue). Melee Weapon Attack: +7
   to hit, reach 5 ft., one target. *Hit:* 8 (1d8 + 4) piercing damage
   plus 7 (2d6) fire damage.

At 36, Baron Scale is a doting husband and father of two small children. His wife, Liera, is the youngest daughter of a distant count, and she and her husband make a highly effective and like-minded pair, working together toward their common goals of peace and prosperity for Cat's Cradle. Starting a family seems to have softened Baron Scale, such that he has become easier to read and more honest about his goals.

This has had the effect of making the man more popular than ever with his people, but his moves have also become easier to predict, and his support among the wealthy and upper classes is slipping. It seems clear to these sections of society that Baron Scale cares more for the poor than the rich and has no interest in larger-scale power games.

The baron and his wife, however, remain charming and courteous at those upper-scale events they feel compelled to attend, and the baron is still a cunning long-term strategist and natural leader, able to manipulate even those who dislike him to make the deals Cat's Cradle needs for its long term prosperity. He dislikes flattery and is well known for his swordplay.

BARON SCALE (CR 10)

Medium human, lawful good

Armor Class 19 (*+2 half plate*)
Hit Points 169 (26d8 + 52)
Speed 30 ft.

STR	DEX	CON	INT	WIS	CHA
13 (+1)	15 (+2)	15 (+2)	16 (+3)	18 (+4)	18 (+4)

Saving Throws Int +7, Wis +7
Skills History +7, Insight +7, Intimidation +8, Investigation +7, Performance (oratory) +8, Persuasion +8
Senses passive Perception 17
Languages Common, Dwarvish, Elvish
Challenge 10 (5900 XP)

Loyal Bodyguards. Baron Scale is constantly accompanied by 2-8 loyal bodyguards (**knights**).

Actions

Multiattack. The Baron makes two Ancestral Rapier attacks.
Ancestral Rapier (rapier +2 flame tongue). Melee Weapon Attack: +8 to hit, reach 5 ft., one target. *Hit:* 8 (1d8+4) piercing damage, plus 7 (2d6) fire damage.

ERROL SYLANNIS

A tall, emaciated man with sallow skin pulls his tattered black robes closer around himself as he moves away from the larger crowds. His bright blue eyes are watery and red-ringed, but dart around with acute attention, soaking in his surroundings. He uses a four-foot rod made of a single piece of bone to prod at some of the wares of a market stall before scowling in the direction of some passing guards, and hurries away.

Errol's life has been filled with tragedy for as long as he could remember. When he was a youth, he and his family were forced to flee their home due to foreign invaders. Those of them that were not butchered were forced into squalor, living in filthy conditions as place after place turned them away. Unfortunately, the family members that survived these harsh times as refugees and finally found a new home soon perished due to sickness. Errol always had a knack for learning new skills and was able to tap into the arcane energies of the universe and had aspirations to one day go and join one of the arcane colleges, but these back-to-back horrible events broke the mind of the young lad. He leaned into this magical aptitude, stealing potions and scrolls in an attempt to either turn back time or to return his fallen family to him… As one could imagine, things did not go well for him. Years later, Errol finds himself in Cat's Cradle. The tales of the power of the salts drew him here, and he looks to add them to his ongoing dark and dangerous experiments.

ERROL SYLVANNIS

Medium humanoid, neutral evil

Armor Class 12 (15 with *mage armor*)

Hit Points 27 (5d8 + 5)
Speed 30 ft.

STR	DEX	CON	INT	WIS	CHA
10 (+0)	15 (+2)	13 (+1)	17 (+3)	13 (+1)	10 (+0)

Saving Throws Int +5, Wis +3
Skills Arcana +5, Medicine +3
Senses passive Perception 11
Languages Common, Draconic, Dwarvish, Elvish
Challenge 3 (700 XP)

Grim Harvest. Once per turn when Errol kills one or more creatures with a spell of 1st level or higher, he regains hit points equal to twice the spell's level, or three times its level if the spell belongs to the School of Necromancy. He doesn't gain this benefit for killing constructs or undead.
Spellcasting. Errol is a 5th-level spellcaster. His spellcasting ability is Intelligence (spell save DC 13, +5 to hit with spell attacks). He has the following wizard spells prepared:
Cantrips (at will): *dancing lights, mage hand, mending, ray of frost*
1st level (4 slots): *detect magic, false life*, mage armor*, ray of sickness*
2nd level (3 slots): *blindness/deafness, gentle repose, invisibility*
3rd level (2 slots): *bestow curse*

Actions

Dagger. Melee or Ranged Weapon Attack: +4 to hit, reach 5 ft. or range 20/60 ft., one target. *Hit:* 4 (1d4 + 2) piercing damage.
Quarterstaff. Melee Weapon Attack: +2 to hit, reach 5 ft., one target. *Hit:* 3 (1d6) bludgeoning damage, or 4 (1d8) bludgeoning damage if used with two hands.

**Errol casts these spells on himself before combat*

Skirting around the city limits, Errol had learned the patrol patterns of the guards and soldiers that gave him the most hassle and avoids them, preferring to enter the city during shift changes or when there are guards on duty who would prefer a simple bribe to let him enter rather than waste their time detaining him. Errol's destinations are always the same: Alchemist's Row and the shop of Jall Krukrich the ratfolk, both for picking up supplies and components of both the arcane and the more unsavory nature. Traveling with him are hooded, cloaked, and enchanted skeletons that act as bodyguards, or as distractions should the occasion arise that Errol needs to make a quick getaway! Use **skeleton**, but with the *minor image* spell permanently cast up on them.

ERROL SYLVANNIS
Medium humanoid, neutral evil

Armor Class 12 (15 with *mage armor*)
Hit Points 65 (10d8 +16)
Speed 30 ft.

STR	DEX	CON	INT	WIS	CHA
10 (+0)	15 (+2)	13 (+1)	18 (+4)	13 (+1)	10 (+0)

Saving Throws Int +7, Wis +4
Skills Arcana +7, History +7, Medicine +4
Damage Resistance necrotic damage
Senses passive Perception 11
Languages Common, Draconic, Dwarvish, Elvish, Infernal
Challenge 6 (2,300 XP)

Grim Harvest. Once per turn when Errol kills one or more creatures with a spell of 1st level or higher, he regains hit points equal to twice the spell's level, or three times its level of the spell belongs to the School of Necromancy. He doesn't gain this benefit for killing constructs or undead.
Servants from the Grave. Errol travels with 1d4 + 2 disguised **skeletons** at all times.
Spellcasting. Errol is a 10th-level spellcaster. His spellcasting ability is Intelligence (spell save DC 15, +7 to hit with spell attacks). He has the following wizard spells prepared:
Cantrips (at will): *dancing lights, mage hand, mending, ray of frost, true strike*
1st level (4 slots): *charm person, detect magic, false life*, mage armor*, ray of sickness*
2nd level (3 slots): *blindness/deafness, gentle repose, invisibility*
3rd level (3 slots): *animate dead, bestow curse, dispel magic*
4th level (3 slots): *blight, secret chest*
5th level (2 slots): *mislead*

Actions

Dagger. *Melee or Ranged Weapon Attack:* +5 to hit, reach 5 ft. or range 20/60 ft., one target. *Hit:* 4 (1d4 + 2) piercing damage.
Quarterstaff. *Melee Weapon Attack:* +3 to hit, reach 5 ft., one target. *Hit:* 3 (1d6) bludgeoning damage, or 4 (1d8) bludgeoning damage if used with two hands.

**Errol casts these spells on himself before combat*

Errol is now situated at the Graveyard of Mur, outside the city of Cat's Cradle, on the way to the Salt Mines (albeit, a bit off the beaten track). While he looks like a withered older man (evidence that his necromantic practices have taken a toll on his general appearance), he is still a vigorous young man in his late 20s, He handles all of the gravedigging and groundskeeping work of the property by himself, preferring to work alone. He finds that people either disapprove of his philosophies, are judgmental of his work, or wish to do him harm. Even though he tends to keep them out of sight as much as he is able, Errol is known to have at least a dozen undead with him at all times. He continues his work for immortality and is constantly seeking rare components, tomes, and spell books that can assist him in his quest.

ERROL SYLVANNIS
Medium humanoid, neutral evil

Armor Class 13 (16 with *mage armor*)
Hit Points 92 (15d8 +21)
Speed 30 ft.

STR	DEX	CON	INT	WIS	CHA
10 (+0)	16 (+3)	13 (+1)	20 (+5)	13 (+1)	10 (+0)

Saving Throws Int +9, Wis +5
Skills Arcana +9, History +9, Medicine +5, Religion +9
Damage Resistance necrotic damage
Senses passive Perception 11
Languages Abyssal, Common, Draconic, Dwarvish, Elvish, Infernal
Challenge 10 (5,900 XP)

Grim Harvest. Once per turn when Errol kills one or more creatures with a spell of 1st level or higher, he regains hit points equal to twice the spell's level, or three times its level of the spell belongs to the School of Necromancy. He doesn't gain this benefit for killing constructs or undead.
Servants from the Grave. Errol travels with 1d4 + 2 disguised **skeletons** at all times. When he is on the grounds of the graveyard, he has an additional 1d4 **zombies** and 1d3 disguised **ghouls** with him as well.
Spellcasting. Errol is a 15th-level spellcaster. His spellcasting ability is Intelligence (spell save DC 17, +9 to hit with spell attacks). He has the following wizard spells prepared:
Cantrips (at will): *dancing lights, mage hand, mending, ray of frost, true strike*
1st level (4 slots): *charm person, detect magic, false life*, mage armor*, ray of sickness*
2nd level (3 slots): *blindness/deafness, gentle repose, invisibility*
3rd level (3 slots): *animate dead, bestow curse, dispel magic*
4th level (3 slots): *blight, secret chest*
5th level (2 slots): *mislead, scrying*
6th level (1 slots): *create undead*
7th level (1 slots): *finger of death*
8th level (1 slots): *clone*

Actions

Multiattack. Errol makes two melee attacks.
Dagger. *Melee or Ranged Weapon Attack:* +7 to hit, reach 5 ft. or range 20/60 ft., one target. *Hit:* 4 (1d4+3) piercing damage.
Quarterstaff. *Melee Weapon Attack:* +4 to hit, reach 5 ft., one target. *Hit:* 3 (1d6) bludgeoning damage, or 4 (1d8) bludgeoning damage.
Command Undead. Errol chooses one undead that he can see within 60 feet of himself. That creature must make a DC 17 Charisma saving throw. If it succeeds, he cannot use this feature on it again. If it fails, it becomes friendly to him and obeys Errol's commands until he uses this feature again.
Intelligent undead are harder to control in this way. If the target has an Intelligence of 8 or higher, it has advantage on the saving throw. If it fails the saving throw and has an Intelligence of 12 or higher, it can repeat the saving throw at the end of every hour until it succeeds and breaks free.

**Errol casts these spells on himself before combat*

FLOYD THE BAKER

The proprietor of the 'Happy Surprise Bakery' in the Gold District of Cat's Cradle is a pleasant portly human man of over average height with light chestnut hair that is starting to go grey. He has bushy, prominent mutton chops down the sides of his face that reach his jawline. Wearing a cook's apron, this human man has a smile on his reddish, ruddy face and a twinkle in his bright green eyes.

Floyd Tarryfoot, or Floyd the Baker to everyone in town, is known for his wonderful fresh bread, his "good spirit" pastries (said to have blessings baked right into them!), and his jovial laugh. While not officially an alchemist or apothecary, he is a cleric and often has a handful of lesser potions for sale in his shop, placed on his immaculate oak countertop right next to the freshly baked cookies. When not inside tending to customers or seeing to his ovens, Floyd sits out on the front stoop of the shop chatting with some of the town locals, a passing guard, or travelers looking for some supplies. He often can be found recounting outlandish tales he has overheard being told by his customers. While he denies being any source of information or even one to further rumors, he always seems to have something ready to tell as he gives a little nudge and wink.

FLOYD THE BAKER

Medium humanoid, chaotic neutral

Armor Class 16 (chain shirt, shield)
Hit Points 32 (5d8 + 10)
Speed 30 ft.

STR	DEX	CON	INT	WIS	CHA
10 (+0)	13 (+1)	14 (+2)	10 (+0)	17 (+3)	15 (+2)

Saving Throws Wis +5, Cha +4
Skills Deception +4, Medicine +5, Persuasion +4, Religion +2
Senses passive Perception 13
Languages Common
Challenge 3 (700 XP)

Innate spellcasting. Floyd's innate spellcasting ability is Wisdom (spell save DC 13). He can innately cast the following spells, requiring no material components, once per day: *charm person, disguise self, mirror image, pass without trace, blink, dispel magic*
Spellcasting. Floyd is a 5th-level spellcaster. His spellcasting ability is Wisdom (spell save DC 13, +5 to hit with spell attacks). He has the following cleric spells prepared:
Cantrips (at will): *guidance, mending, sacred flame, thaumaturgy*
1st level (4 slots): *bless, charm person, disguise self, healing word, purify food and drink*
2nd level (3 slots): *lesser restoration, mirror image, pass without trace, silence*
3rd level (2 slots): *blink, dispel magic, sending, tongues*

Actions

Mace. *Melee Weapon Attack:* +2 to hit, reach 5 ft., one target. *Hit:* 3 (1d6) bludgeoning damage.
Crossbow, Light. *Ranged Weapon Attack:* +3 to hit, range 80/320 ft., one target. *Hit:* 5 (1d8 + 1) piercing damage.
Trickster's Deception. Floyd can attempt to deceive and hide from anyone that can see him. All creatures that can see Floyd must make a DC 14 Wisdom saving throw. If successful, there is no effect. Any creatures that fail treat Floyd as if he was invisible until the end of his next turn. Floyd loses his invisibility to a target if he attacks them or casts a spell on them.

After a lengthy renovation period of his shop (which the player may or may not have been roped into by their friendly neighborhood baker), the Happy Surprise Baker has reopened and is better than ever! With glass window displays showing off his fresh baked goods, racks of sugars, spices, and potions, and tables both inside and out to have warm drinks, the place is a welcoming haven. Unbeknownst to anyone, Floyd has set up a shrine underneath the shop in devotion to his deity: Loki, the god of mischief and trickery. A devout follower, Floyd has worked for years to master the arts of deception, misinformation, and practical jokes. While he never intentionally performs these duties with malice or harm in his heart, he gets no greater joy than leading someone astray or causing a mishap. Maybe it was a swapped potion label, or serving decaf instead of a caffeinated beverage, or maybe that rumor that illegal goods were being shipped in through slip four at midnight wasn't completely up-to-snuff. In any event, Floyd gets a good laugh, and at the end of the day, no one gets hurt.

FLOYD THE BAKER

Medium humanoid, chaotic neutral

Armor Class 16 (chain shirt, shield)
Hit Points 65 (10d8 + 20)
Speed 30 ft.

STR	DEX	CON	INT	WIS	CHA
10 (+0)	13 (+1)	14 (+2)	10 (+0)	18 (+4)	16 (+3)

Saving Throws Wis +7, Cha +6
Skills Deception +6, Medicine +7, Persuasion +6, Religion +3
Senses passive Perception 14
Languages Common
Challenge 6 (2,300 XP)

Divine Strike. Once per turn, when Floyd hits a creature with a weapon attack, he can cause the attack to deal an additional 1d8 poison damage to the target.
Innate spellcasting. Floyd's innate spellcasting ability is Wisdom (spell save DC 15). He can innately cast the following spells, requiring no material components, once per day: *charm person, disguise self, mirror image, pass without trace, blink, dispel magic, polymorph, dominate person, modify memory*
Spellcasting. Floyd is a 10th-level spellcaster. His spellcasting ability is Wisdom (spell save DC 15, +7 to hit with spell attacks). He has the following cleric spells prepared:
Cantrips (at will): *guidance, mending, sacred flame, thaumaturgy*
1st level (4 slots): *bless, charm person, disguise self, healing word, purify food and drink*
2nd level (3 slots): *lesser restoration, mirror image, pass without trace, silence*
3rd level (3 slots): *blink, dispel magic, feign death, sending, tongues*
4th level (3 slots): *dimension door, freedom of movement, locate creature, polymorph**
5th level (2 slots): *dominate person, modify memory, scrying*

Actions

Mace. *Melee Weapon Attack:* +3 to hit, reach 5 ft., one target. *Hit:* 3 (1d6) bludgeoning damage.
Crossbow, Light. *Ranged Weapon Attack:* +4 to hit, range 80/320 ft., one target. *Hit:* 5 (1d8 + 1) piercing damage.

Trickster's Deception. Floyd can attempt to deceive and hide from anyone that can see him. All creatures that can see Floyd must make a DC 16 Wisdom saving throw. If successful, there is no effect. Any creatures that fail treat Floyd as if he was invisible until the end of his next turn. Floyd loses his invisibility to a target if he attacks them or casts a spell on them.

At the behest of his patreon deity, Floyd has expanded his misinformation giving into a side job to his thriving bakery business. Never wanting the trail to make its way back to him, Floyd has started forging bounty notices, help wanted posters, lost item requests, and missing people reports that he has posted all over town. Not only that, but one in four of his potions are now diluted to either last only half the normal length, or only perform half the desired effect. While he continues with the mindset that he doesn't want any serious harm to come to anyone, he always makes sure to sprinkle a little bit of truth in all of his tricks. Floyd knows that he is starting to cross a dangerous line when it comes to his mischief, but he can't help but find it all so terribly funny.

FLOYD THE BAKER

Medium humanoid, chaotic neutral

Hit Points 97 (15d8 + 30)
Speed 30 ft.

STR	DEX	CON	INT	WIS	CHA
10 (+0)	13 (+1)	14 (+2)	10 (+0)	18 (+4)	18 (+4)

Saving Throws Wis +8, Cha +8
Skills Deception +8, Medicine +8, Persuasion +8, Religion +4
Senses passive Perception 14
Languages Common
Challenge 10 (5,900 XP)

Divine Strike. Once per turn, when Floyd hits a creature with a weapon attack, he can cause the attack to deal an additional 2d8 poison damage to the target.

Innate spellcasting. Floyd's innate spellcasting ability is Wisdom (spell save DC 16). He can innately cast the following spells, requiring no material components, once per day: *charm person, disguise self, mirror image, pass without trace, blink, dispel magic, polymorph, dominate person, modify memory*

Spellcasting. Floyd is a 15th-level spellcaster. His spellcasting ability is Wisdom (spell save DC 16, +8 to hit with spell attacks). He has the following cleric spells prepared:
Cantrips (at will): *guidance, mending, sacred flame, thaumaturgy*
1st level (4 slots): *bless, charm person, disguise self, healing word, purify food and drink*
2nd level (3 slots): *lesser restoration, mirror image, pass without trace, silence*
3rd level (3 slots): *blink, dispel magic, feign death, sending, tongues*
4th level (3 slots): *dimension door, freedom of movement, locate creature, polymorph*
5th level (2 slots): *dominate person, modify memory, scrying*
6th level (1 slots): *true seeing*
7th level (1 slots): *plane shift*
8th level (1 slots): *control weather*

Actions

Multiattack. Floyd makes two melee attacks.
Mace. Melee Weapon Attack: +4 to hit, reach 5 ft., one target. *Hit:* 3 (1d6) bludgeoning damage.
Crossbow, Light. Ranged Weapon Attack: +5 to hit, range 80/320 ft., one target. *Hit:* 5 (1d8 + 1) piercing damage.
Trickster's Deception. Floyd can attempt to deceive and hide from anyone that can see him. All creatures that can see Floyd must make a DC 18 wisdom saving throw. If successful, there is no effect. Any creatures that fail treat Floyd as if he was invisible until the end of his next turn. Floyd loses his invisibility to a target if he attacks them or casts a spell on them.

GARRON THORN

One of the Kennick Syndicate's most trusted operatives in the Ovens District, Garron Thorn is a halfling whose character is made of equal parts ruthlessness and cunning. A rising star with the Syndicate, Thorn leads a crew of 20 or so low-level soldiers who specialize in protection, extortion, and petty robbery. His self-applied nickname "The Boss of Bricktown" has begun to catch on, earning him even more notoriety in the eyes of Old Man Kennick.

Thorn is outwardly an unassuming halfling who dresses modestly and seems relatively ordinary save for the well-used shortsword at his side. Though his overall demeanor is calm and can be quite garrulous and even friendly, Thorn is infamous for his fiery temper, which can explode into acts of appalling violence — mercilessly beating victims, engaging in the torture of those who have resisted his gang's protection rackets, and even nailing the limbs and heads of disloyal minions to the floor. Thorn's cruelty has created a cult of both fear and respect, as he allows only the most fanatical and loyal of Kennick operatives to join his growing organization.

GARRON THORN (CR 3)

Medium humanoid (halfling), neutral evil

Armor Class 15 (breastplate)
Hit Points 77 (14d8 + 14)
Speed 25 ft.

STR	DEX	CON	INT	WIS	CHA
15 (+2)	13 (+1)	12 (+1)	11 (+0)	15 (+2)	14 (+2)

Saving Throws Wis +4, Cha +5
Skills Deception +4, Insight +4, Intimidation +4, Perception +4, Persuasion +4, Sleight of Hand +3, Stealth +3
Senses passive Perception 14
Languages Common, Gnomish, Halfling
Challenge 3 (700 XP)

Brave. Garron Thorn has advantage on saving throws against being frightened.

Brutal. Garron Thorn has advantage on Charisma (Intimidation) checks.

Halfling Nimbleness. Thorn can move through the space of any creature that is of a size larger than him.

Naturally Stealthy. Thorn can attempt to hide even if obscured only by a creature that is at least one size larger than him.

Actions

Shortsword. *Melee Weapon Attack:* +4 to hit, reach 5 ft., one target. *Hit:* 5 (1d6 + 2) piercing damage

Light Crossbow. *Ranged Weapon Attack:* +3 to hit, range 80/320 ft., one target. *Hit:* 7 (1d8 + 3) piercing damage

The Boss of Brickton has fully earned his moniker and now he controls a small army of thugs and operatives as Old Man Kennick's most trusted subordinate. He dresses in grey and black, and habitually wears a broad-brimmed black hat pulled low over his eyes. He has grown smarter, crueler, and even more clever, but with his successes have come troubles as well. Ensconced in a well-protected home in the heart of the Ovens, Garron Thorn is intensely jealous of his power, and increasingly fearful of competition from other aspiring gang leaders. He has also developed a deep fear of the water — a liability in a lake city like Cat's Cradle. He particularly fears the serpents that lurk in the deep water, and a single monster he calls only "Winston" in particular. Some of Thorn's associates feel that he is losing his mind, and that "Winston" is nothing but a figment of his imagination.

GARRON THORN (CR 6)

Small humanoid (halfling), neutral evil

Armor Class 15 (breastplate)
Hit Points 110 (20d8 + 20)
Speed 25 ft.

STR	DEX	CON	INT	WIS	CHA
15 (+2)	14 (+2)	12 (+1)	12 (+1)	16 (+3)	14 (+2)

Saving Throws Wis +5, Cha +6
Skills Deception +5, Insight +6, Intimidation +5, Perception +6, Persuasion +5, Sleight of Hand +5, Stealth +5
Senses passive Perception 16
Languages Common, Gnomish, Halfling
Challenge 6 (2300 XP)

Brave. Garron Thorn has advantage on saving throws against being frightened.

Brutal. Garron Thorn has advantage on Charisma (Intimidation) checks.

Halfling Nimbleness. Thorn can move through the space of any creature that is of a size larger than him.

Naturally Stealthy. Thorn can attempt to hide even if obscured only by a creature that is at least one size larger than him.

Actions

+2 Poisoned Shortsword. *Melee Weapon Attack:* +7 to hit, reach 5 ft., one target. *Hit:* 7 (1d6 + 4) piercing damage, and the target must succeed on a DC 15 Constitution saving throw or be poisoned for 1 hour.

Light Crossbow. *Ranged Weapon Attack:* +5 to hit, range 80/320 ft., one target. *Hit:* 7 (1d8 + 3) piercing damage

At the height of his power, Thorn is the undisputed gang chief of the Ovens, but his crippling paranoia and fear keeps him in his fortified residence, from which he oversees Syndicate operations, issuing orders, disciplining subordinates, and meting out justice to turncoats or uncooperative shopkeepers. He has avoided arrest by the Watch and by those members of the Constabulary determined to bring him to justice, yet he grows increasingly fearful, still afraid of the lake and the ever-present "Winston", whom he claims watches him through his windows at night.

GARRON THORN

Small humanoid (halfling), neutral evil

Armor Class 17 (+2 breastplate)
Hit Points 165 (30d8 + 30)
Speed 25 ft.

STR	DEX	CON	INT	WIS	CHA
15 (+2)	14 (+2)	12 (+1)	12 (+1)	16 (+3)	16 (+3)

Saving Throws Wis +5, Cha +6
Skills Deception +7, Insight +7, Intimidation +7, Perception +7, Persuasion +7, Sleight of Hand +6, Stealth +6
Senses passive Perception 17
Languages Common, Gnomish, Halfling
Challenge 10 (5900 XP)

Brave. Garron Thorn has advantage on saving throws against being frightened.

Brutal. Garron Thorn has advantage on Charisma (Intimidation) checks.

Halfling Nimbleness. Thorn can move through the space of any creature that is of a size larger than him.

Naturally Stealthy. Thorn can attempt to hide even if obscured only by a creature that is at least one size larger than him.

Actions

+2 Poisoned Shortsword. *Melee Weapon Attack:* +8 to hit, reach 5 ft., one target. *Hit:* 7 (1d6 + 4) piercing damage, and the target must succeed on a DC 15 Constitution saving throw or be poisoned for 1 hour.

Light Crossbow. *Ranged Weapon Attack:* +6 to hit, range 80/320 ft., one target. *Hit:* 7 (1d8 + 3) piercing damage

HELEZIA ARREN

An accomplished spellcaster in her hometown, Helezia Arren ventured to Cat's Cradle in the hope of learning the trade of alchemy at the city college. Despite her magical accomplishment, the college's fees proved exorbitant, forcing her into work as a freelance spellcaster and occasional adventurer, as well as serving as an assistant to her instructors in exchange for discounted tuition. She has taken to her classes with enthusiasm, prompting her instructors to describe her as a natural talent, and if encountered will always be carrying 2d6 randomly-determined potions or alchemical substances (see Appendix B).

Helezia is quietly obsessed with her science, to the extent that she doesn't pay much attention to her appearance or keeping her garments in order, and presents herself as a somewhat wild-haired, intense-eyed woman clad in modest garments more suited to a country villager than a skilled wizard and aspiring alchemist. Despite her eccentricities — or perhaps because of them — she is popular with adventurers and other transient, knockabout types, who appreciate her presence on explorations or dungeon delves, where she is far more interested in collecting rare substances and potions than in gold and other traditional treasures.

HELEZIA ARREN

Medium humanoid (human), neutral good

Armor Class 12 (15 with *mage armor*)
Hit Points 55 (10d8 + 10)
Speed 30 ft.

STR	DEX	CON	INT	WIS	CHA
11 (+0)	14 (+2)	12 (+1)	18 (+4)	14 (+2)	12 (+1)

Saving Throws Constitution +3, Intelligence +6
Skills Arcana +6, History +6, Medicine +4
Senses passive Perception 12
Languages Common, Draconic, Dwarvish, Elvish
Challenge 3 (700 XP)

Spellcasting. Helezia is a 6th-level spellcaster. Her spellcasting ability is Intelligence (spell save DC 14, +6 to hit with spell attacks). She has the following wizard spells prepared:

Cantrips (at will): *acid splash, fire bolt, mage hand, mending*
1st level (4 slots): *burning hands, grease, mage armor, unseen servant*
2nd level (3 slots): *continual flame, enlarge/reduce, shatter*
3rd level (3 slots): *gaseous form, fireball, stinking cloud*

Actions

Shortsword. *Melee Weapon Attack*: +4 to hit, reach 5 ft., one target. *Hit*: 5 (1d6 + 2) piercing damage.

In her third year at the college, Helezia continues to grow and evolve into a skilled alchemist. She earns significant income from sales of her various products, both through Academy Sales and on her own. Her popularity as an adventuring companion has grown as well, and now she is finding her schedule starting to get crowded as she divides her time between class and dungeoneering. Her potions are more potent now, further adding to her popularity.

HELEZIA ARREN

Medium humanoid (human), neutral good

Armor Class 12 (15 with *mage armor*)
Hit Points 77 (14d8 + 14)
Speed 30 ft.

STR	DEX	CON	INT	WIS	CHA
11 (+0)	14 (+2)	12 (+1)	18 (+4)	14 (+2)	12 (+1)

Saving Throws Constitution +4, Intelligence +7
Skills Arcana +7, History +7, Medicine +5
Senses passive Perception 12
Languages Common, Draconic, Dwarvish, Elvish
Challenge 6 (2300 XP)

Spellcasting. Helezia is an 8th-level spellcaster. Her spellcasting ability is Intelligence (spell save DC 15, +7 to hit with spell attacks). She has the following wizard spells prepared:

1st level (4 slots): *burning hands, grease, mage armor, unseen servant*
2nd level (3 slots): *continual flame, enlarge/reduce, shatter*
3rd level (3 slots): *gaseous form, fireball, stinking cloud*
4th level (2 slots): *control water, stone shape*

Actions

Shortsword. *Melee Weapon Attack*: +5 to hit, reach 5 ft., one target. *Hit*: 5 (1d6 + 2) piercing damage.

On the verge of graduation, Helezia has been the head of the Alchemical Students' Organization for a year now and contemplates taking employment as a part-time instructor at the college. Though she still occasionally ventures out of Cat's Cradle with adventurers, she more frequently employs them herself, sending them out to obtain rare and important ingredients.

HELEZIA ARREN

Medium humanoid (human), neutral good

Armor Class 12 (15 with *mage armor*)
Hit Points 88 (16d8 + 16)
Speed 30 ft.

STR	DEX	CON	INT	WIS	CHA
11 (+0)	14 (+2)	12 (+1)	19 (+4)	14 (+2)	12 (+1)

Saving Throws Constitution +5, Intelligence +8
Skills Arcana +8, History +8, Medicine +6
Senses passive Perception 12
Languages Common, Draconic, Dwarvish, Elvish
Challenge 10 (5900 XP)

Spellcasting. Helezia is an 10th-level spellcaster. Her spellcasting ability is Intelligence (spell save DC 16, +8 to hit with spell attacks). She has the following wizard spells prepared:

1st level (4 slots): *burning hands, grease, mage armor, unseen servant*
2nd level (3 slots): *continual flame, enlarge/reduce, shatter*
3rd level (3 slots): *gaseous form, fireball, stinking cloud*
4th level (3 slots): *control water, fabricate, stone shape*
5th level (2 slots): *conjure elemental, creation*

Actions

Shortsword. *Melee Weapon Attack*: +6 to hit, reach 5 ft., one target. *Hit*: 5 (1d6 + 2) piercing damage.

HENRIC HAMMERHILL

A stout dwarven man with dark skin and a long black beard he keeps braided and clasped to his studded leather jerkin. His shaven head is kept covered not only with his hooded cloak, but also with a leather cap inscribed with a bird of prey. While seemingly like any other dwarf at first glance, he is surprisingly more agile and stealthy than his slower moving, stocky brethren. When springing into combat, he either dual wields a shortsword and handaxe, fires his elaborately engraved shortbow, or swings his mithril-headed maul.

Relatively new to Cat's Cradle, Henric Hammerhill came into the region from the west riding a dwarven war ram and accompanied by his only friend and companion, a black and red feathered axe beak by the name of Muuaji. Without a silver to his name, he has begun hiring his services out to the locals in exchange for coin when he can get it (or food, drink, and lodging when he cannot). While not yet familiar with the surrounding terrain, Henric is a skilled survivalist and hunter, and has begun to earn the reputation of being reliable and honest, sure to keep a level head in tense situations and be a voice of reason. Whether it be helping track something in the wilds, providing an extra blade in battle, or guarding people along the trade routes in and out of

town, the stoic Henric Hammerhill is willing to do just about anything within his skill set for pay.

HENRIC HAMMERHILL

Medium humanoid, lawful neutral

Armor Class 15 (studded leather)
Hit Points 52 (8d8 + 16)
Speed 30 ft.

STR	DEX	CON	INT	WIS	CHA
16 (+3)	17 (+3)	15 (+2)	13 (+1)	16 (+3)	12 (+1)

Saving Throws Str +5, Dex +5
Skills Animal Handling +3, Insight +3, Investigation +5, Nature +3, Perception +5, Survival +5
Senses passive Perception 15
Languages Common, Dwarvish, Goblin
Challenge 3 (700 XP)

Animal Companion. Henric is bonded to Muuaji, an **axe beak**, which is his animal companion. The companion acts on its own initiative, but otherwise obeys Henric's commands. As a bonus action, Henric can command Muuaji to use its reaction to take the Dash, Disengage, Dodge, or Help action.
Brave. Henric has advantage on saving throws against being frightened.
Colossus Slayer (1/turn). When Henric hits a creature with a weapon attack, the creature takes an extra 1d8 damage if it's below its hit point maximum.
Spellcasting. Henric is an 8th-level spellcaster. His spellcasting ability is Wisdom (spell save DC 13, +5 to hit with spell attacks). He has the following ranger spells:
1st level (4 slots): *detect magic, ensnaring strike, speak with animals*
2nd level (3 slots): *beast sense, pass without trace*

Actions

Multiattack. Henric makes two melee attacks.
Shortsword. *Melee Weapon Attack:* +5 to hit, reach 5 ft., one target. *Hit:* 6 (1d6 + 3) piercing damage.
Handaxe. *Melee or Ranged Weapon Attack:* +5 to hit, reach 5 ft. or range 20/60 ft., one target. *Hit:* 6 (1d6 + 3) slashing damage.
Mithril Maul. *Melee Weapon Attack:* +5 to hit, reach 5 ft., one target. *Hit:* 10 (2d6 + 3) bludgeoning damage.
Shortbow. *Ranged Weapon Attack:* +5 to hit, range 30/120 ft., one target. *Hit:* 6 (1d6 + 3) piercing damage

One of the prominent hunters and trackers in the region, Henric Hammerhill can usually be found sitting quietly on the porch of one of the better known taverns or inns in town. Accompanying him nearby (or sometimes even at his table, making a mess and eating bits of leftover venison) is his **axe beak** companion Muuaji. Both dwarf and large bird watch passersby with a modicum of interest, content in their solitude but ready for any job should the opportunity present itself. Henric often provides guidance to those new to the area and need to get their bearing when traversing the surrounding wilderness, but also provides game to the local food merchants (sanctioned by the city lords, of course).

As most of his time is dedicated toward official hunting trips or for performing escort missions, Henric is always in need of people to handle a few odd jobs for him. He may require a package of meat to be delivered to an out-of-the-way client, or perhaps pick up a bundle of expensive hides from a furrier who has had some bandit trouble of late. On a more personal note, Hammerhill is looking for someone who can track down and handle a tribe of goblins in the nearby forest who have been rumored to be training owlbears to aid in their harassment of other rangers, woodsmen, and even miners in the region.

HENRIC HAMMERHILL

Medium humanoid, lawful neutral

Armor Class 15 (chain shirt)
Hit Points 82 (12d8 + 24)
Speed 30 ft.

STR	DEX	CON	INT	WIS	CHA
16 (+3)	18 (+4)	15 (+2)	13 (+1)	16 (+3)	12 (+1)

Saving Throws Str +6, Dex +7
Skills Animal Handling +4, Insight +6, Investigation +4, Nature +4, Perception +6, Survival +6
Senses passive Perception 16
Languages Common, Dwarvish, Goblin
Challenge 6 (2,300 XP)

Animal Companion. Henric is bonded to Muuaji, an **axe beak**, which is his animal companion. The companion acts on its own initiative, but otherwise obeys Henric's commands. As a bonus action, Henric can command Muuaji to use its reaction to take the Dash, Disengage, Dodge, or Help action.
Brave. Henric has advantage on saving throws against being frightened.
Colossus Slayer (1/turn). When Henric hits a creature with a weapon attack, the creature takes an extra 1d8 damage if it's below its hit point maximum.
Spellcasting. Henric is a 12th-level spellcaster. His spellcasting ability is Wisdom (spell save DC 14, +6 to hit with spell attacks). He has the following ranger spells:
1st level (4 slots): *detect magic, ensnaring strike, speak with animals*
2nd level (3 slots): *beast sense, pass without trace*
3rd level (3 slots): *nondetection, lightning arrow*

Actions

Multiattack. Henric makes two melee attacks.
Shortsword. *Melee Weapon Attack:* +7 to hit, reach 5 ft., one target. *Hit:* 7 (1d6 + 4) piercing damage.
Handaxe. *Melee or Ranged Weapon Attack:* +7 to hit, reach 5 ft. or range 20/60 ft., one target. *Hit:* 7 (1d6 + 4) slashing damage.

Mithril Maul. Melee Weapon Attack: +6 to hit, reach 5 ft., one
target. *Hit:* 10 (2d6 + 3) bludgeoning damage.

Shortbow. Ranged Weapon Attack: +7 to hit, range 30/120 ft., one
target. *Hit:* 7 (1d6 + 4) piercing damage

Volley. Henric may make a ranged attack against any number of
creatures within 10 feet of a point he can see within his weapon's
range. He must make a separate attack roll for each target.

Henric Hammerhill has become a bit of a recluse during the course of the
last few years. While still known as one of the premiere hunters and trackers of
the region, he no longer attends the court nor offers his services to anyone since
the deaths of his family at the hands (or more accurately: claws and fangs) of
Jokulvargr, an awakened demonic winter wolf. Henric has all but retired, keeping
to himself at his cabin in the woods outside of Cat's Cradle, still accompanied
by his **axe beak** Muuaji. In actuality though, Henric seeks out knowledge and
allies in order to one day mount an expedition to the extradimensional home
plane where Jokulvargr resides, along with her pack, the Burning Frost Tribe.
Information, equipment, and magic for planar travel is what Henric now seeks
to obtain, and he will pay handsomely for any brought to him.

HENRIC HAMMERHILL

Medium humanoid, lawful neutral

Armor Class 17 (*+1 breastplate*)
Hit Points 104 (16d8 + 32)
Speed 30 ft.

STR	DEX	CON	INT	WIS	CHA
16 (+3)	18 (+4)	15 (+2)	13 (+1)	18 (+4)	12 (+1)

Saving Throws Str +7, Dex+8
Skills Animal Handling +1, Insight +4, Investigation +8, Nature
+5, Perception +8, Survival +8
Senses passive Perception 18
Languages Common, Dwarvish, Goblin
Challenge 10 (5,900 XP)

Animal Companion. Henric is bonded to Muuaji, an **axe beak**,
which is his animal companion. The companion acts on its own
initiative, but otherwise obeys Henric's commands. As a bonus
action, Henric can command Muuaji to use its reaction to take
the Dash, Disengage, Dodge, or Help action.

Brave. Henric has advantage on saving throws against being
frightened.

Colossus Slayer **(1/turn).** When Henric hits a creature with a
weapon attack, the creature takes an extra 1d8 damage if it's
below its hit point maximum.

Evasion. If Henric is subjected to an effect that allows him to
make a Dexterity saving throw to take only half damage, Henric
instead takes no damage if he succeeds on the saving throw, and
only half damage if he fails.

Spellcasting. Henric is a 16th-level spellcaster. His spellcasting
ability is Wisdom (spell save DC 16, +8 to hit with spell attacks).
He has the following ranger spells:
1st level (4 slots): *detect magic, ensnaring strike, speak with
animals*
2nd level (3 slots): *beast sense, pass without trace*
3rd level (3 slots): *nondetection, lightning arrow*
4th level (2 slots): *freedom of movement, locate creature*

Actions

Multiattack. Henric makes two melee attacks.

Shortsword. Melee Weapon Attack: +8 to hit, reach 5 ft., one
target. *Hit:* 7 (1d6 + 4) piercing damage.

Handaxe. Melee or Ranged Weapon Attack: +8 to hit, reach 5 ft. or
range 20/60 ft., one target. *Hit:* 7 (1d6 + 4) slashing damage.

Mithril Maul. Melee Weapon Attack: +7 to hit, reach 5 ft., one
target. *Hit:* 10 (2d6 + 3) bludgeoning damage.

Shortbow. Ranged Weapon Attack: +8 to hit, range 30/120 ft., one
target. *Hit:* 7 (1d6 + 4) piercing damage

Volley. Henric may make a ranged attack against any number of
creatures within 10 feet of a point he can see within his weapon's
range. He must make a separate attack roll for each target.

JALL KUKRICH

*Though his wiry body is taller by about six inches, Jall Kukrich's hunched
stature marks him as just over four-foot-six. He does his best to keep his black
and grey fur clean by washing from unoccupied watering troughs and keeping
his facial fur and whiskers slicked back with a bit of wagon wheel axle grease he
keeps in a tiny glass jar. He wears an odd, ill-fitting outfit that consists of an old
nobleman's long cape sewn together with both a discarded entertainer's outfit and
some clergyman's robes. Atop his head he wears his most prized possession: an
immaculate crushed velvet red fez, complete with black and gold threaded tassel.
Unlike the rest of his attire, his headpiece is always clean and sits at such a perfect
angle passersby cannot help but smile at Jall when they see him wearing it.*

Like most ratfolk in the Lost Lands, Jall has been a bit of an outcast within
the city since his early days. Arriving by river on a raft made of sticks and
muck, he began working odd jobs at the docks, everything from assisting
fishermen to moving crates and barrels to standing guard at warehouses. But
while he worked hard, he was really keeping his ear to the ground, learning
what he could about the city and its residents: whispers, rumors, stories, deals,
schedules — any bit of information he could turn around and tell interested
parties for a bit of coin. Jall has befriended the young street urchins and
unnoticed youths of the city to help him learn more and further out, created a
loose information network throughout the Docks, Old Town, and the Ovens.
He himself is also looking for any kind of odd job that can either earn him a bit
of coin, or something of value (assuming he is not risking his life, or anything
else dangerous like that!)

JALL KUKRICH

Medium humanoid, chaotic neutral

Armor Class 14 (leather)
Hit Points 36 (8d8)
Speed 30 ft., climb 30 ft.

STR	DEX	CON	INT	WIS	CHA
11 (+0)	16 (+3)	11 (+0)	14 (+2)	15 (+2)	19 (+4)

Saving Throws Dex +5, Cha +6
Skills Acrobatics +5, Deception +8, Insight +4, Perception +4,
Persuasion +8, Sleight of Hand +5, Stealth +5
Damage Resistances poison
Senses darkvision 60ft., passive Perception 14
Languages Common, Dwarvish, Elvish
Challenge 3 (700 XP)

Charming Fez. In addition to granting him a +2 bonus to his
Charisma score (included above), Jall's fez gives him the ability
to cast certain spells. His spellcasting ability is Charisma (spell
save DC 14). The fez allows him to cast the following spells,
requiring no material components:
At will: *detect magic*
3/day: *charm person, suggestion*
1/day: *modify memory*

Cunning Action. On each of his turns, Jall can use a bonus action
to take the Dash, Disengage, or Hide action.

Disease Resistant. Jall has advantage on saving throws against
disease and poison.

Sneak Attack **(1/turn).** Jall deals an extra 7 (2d6) damage when
he hits a target with a weapon attack and has advantage on the
attack roll, or when the target is within 5 feet of an ally of theirs
that isn't incapacitated and Jall doesn't have disadvantage on
the attack roll.

Special Equipment. Jall wears the *charming fez* (see above).
Without the fez, his Charisma is 17.

Actions

Claw and Tooth. Melee Weapon Attack: +5 to hit, reach 5 ft., one
target. *Hit:* 5 (1d4 + 3) slashing damage.

Scimitar. Melee Weapon Attack: +5 to hit, reach 5 ft., one target.
Hit: 6 (1d6 + 3) slashing damage.

Hand Crossbow. Ranged Weapon Attack: +5 to hit, reach 30/120
ft., one target. *Hit:* 6 (1d6 + 3) piercing damage.

You can usually hear the bell tinkling on the covered two-wheeled cart Jall is pulling behind him before you see his fez-adorned smiling rodent face. He moves his moderately-sized "establishment" throughout the Docks, Old Town, the Ovens, and even the southern and eastern areas of the Gold District, calling out to new travelers and adventurers he sees or to citizens he has come to know over the years. Jall's mobile shop sells a variety of goods and items and he is always looking to make a trade, even if he has to offer a discount. However, information is what he deals with more: Do you need dirt on what the corrupt guardsman Sergeant Donovon is handling these days? Or what time a Gold District shopkeep locks up shop and goes home for the night? Perhaps you are wanting to know the latest rumors of the gemstone vein discovered in one of the Salt Mines? These types of things are what Jall excels at knowing and selling, as his network of little spies and information gatherers has grown exponentially. He now has information from all over the city of Cat's Cradle and the surrounding area, even as far as the village of Gambit. However, information has a price, and while gold is always nice, offering up substantiated intel on something Jall doesn't know is preferred.

JALL KUKRICH

Medium humanoid, chaotic neutral

Armor Class 15 (studded leather)
Hit Points 58 (12d8)
Speed 30 ft., climb 30 ft.

STR	DEX	CON	INT	WIS	CHA
11 (+0)	16 (+3)	11 (+0)	14 (+2)	16 (+3)	19 (+4)

Saving Throws Dex +6, Cha +7
Skills Acrobatics +6, Deception +10, Insight +6, Perception +6, Persuasion +10, Sleight of Hand +6, Stealth +6
Damage Resistances poison
Senses darkvision 60ft., passive Perception 16
Languages Common, Dwarvish, Elvish
Challenge 6 (2,300 XP)

> ## WHAT A DEAL!
>
> Consider Jall's mobile cart and The Memorable Fez shop to be a combination of a general store, a potion shop and a weapon vendor, with a fifty percent chance of having what the players are looking for. That being said, for every item Jall doesn't have, immediately offer an item of similar price and style that he actually does have in stock (within reason, at your discretion).
>
> Example: the player is looking for a *potion of healing*. They fail the roll to see if he has it in stock, but Jall immediately points out that he has a *potion of resistance* on his shelf!

Charming Fez. In addition to granting him a +2 bonus to his Charisma score (included above), Jall's fez gives him the ability to cast certain spells. His spellcasting ability is Charisma (spell save DC 15). The fez allows him to cast the following spells, requiring no material components:
At will: *detect magic*
3/day: *charm person, suggestion*
1/day: *modify memory*
Cunning Action. On each of his turns, Jall can use a bonus action to take the Dash, Disengage, Hide or Use an Object action.
Disease Resistant. Jall has advantage on saving throws against disease and poison.
Sneak Attack (1/turn). Jall deals an extra 10 (3d6) damage when he hits a target with a weapon attack and has advantage on the attack roll, or when the target is within 5 feet of an ally of theirs that isn't incapacitated and Jall doesn't have disadvantage on the attack roll.
Special Equipment. Jall wears the *charming fez* (see above). Without the fez, his Charisma is 17.

Actions

Claw and Tooth. *Melee Weapon Attack:* +6 to hit, reach 5 ft., one target. *Hit:* 5 (1d4 + 3) slashing damage.
Scimitar. *Melee Weapon Attack:* +6 to hit, reach 5 ft., one target. *Hit:* 6 (1d6 + 3) slashing damage.
Hand Crossbow. *Ranged Weapon Attack:* +6 to hit, reach 30/120 ft., one target. *Hit:* 6 (1d6 + 3) piercing damage.

Reactions

Uncanny Dodge. Jall can halve the damage of an attack against him. To do so, he must see the attacker.

Situated in the southern area of the Gold District, close to Old Town, Jall owns and runs a small bazaar shop he calls The Memorable Fez where he continues to sell a variety of items of all sorts. In addition to continuing to maintain his information network acquired from the city's underclass youths, Jall has branched out into employing pickpockets, burglars, and forgers. Not only providing requested information, he now offers documents, disguises and uniforms, and even official crests and badges (given the appropriate amount of time and money). As he has always been, Jall is not a violent creature by nature, but is willing to pay top dollar for anyone willing to acquire the things he needs, by any means necessary. Having come a long way from being the damp rat standing on a pier in the Docks, he will do anything to keep what he has built up all these years (including working with the city guard and officials if need be). He pays a contribution to the city guard "retirement fund" every other week to not only be passed along information, but also for them to keep out of his affairs. In addition, he donates a weekly "tithe" to the Temple of Freya to stay in their good graces, even though he doesn't put any stock into the gods. While Jall asserts that he is a master of his own fate, he still appreciates a good blessing or healing from clerics when in need!

JALL KUKRICH

Medium humanoid, chaotic neutral

Armor Class 16 (chain shirt)
Hit Points 72 (16d8)
Speed 30 ft., climb 30 ft.

STR	DEX	CON	INT	WIS	CHA
11 (+0)	16 (+3)	11 (+0)	14 (+2)	16 (+3)	20 (+5)

Saving Throws Dex +7, Cha +9
Skills Acrobatics +7, Deception +13, Insight +7, Perception +7, Persuasion +13, Sleight of Hand +7, Stealth +7
Damage Resistances poison
Senses darkvision 60ft., passive Perception 17
Languages Common, Dwarvish, Elvish
Challenge 10 (5,900 XP)

Charming Fez. In addition to granting him a +2 bonus to his Charisma score (included above), Jall's fez gives him the ability to cast certain spells. His spellcasting ability is Charisma (spell save DC 17). The fez allows him to cast the following spells, requiring no material components:
At will: *detect magic*
3/day: *charm person, suggestion*
1/day: *modify memory*
Cunning Action. On each of his turns, Jall can use a bonus action to take the Dash, Disengage, Hide or Use an Object action.
Disease Resistant. Jall has advantage on saving throws against disease and poison.
Evasion. If Jall is subjected to an effect that allows him to make a Dexterity saving throw to take only half damage, Jall instead takes no damage if he succeeds on the saving throw, and only half damage if he fails.
Sneak Attack (1/turn). Jall deals an extra 14 (4d6) damage when he hits a target with a weapon attack and has advantage on the attack roll, or when the target is within 5 feet of an ally of theirs that isn't incapacitated and Jall doesn't have disadvantage on the attack roll.
Special Equipment. Jall wears the *charming fez* (see above). Without the fez, his Charisma is 18.

Actions

Claw and Tooth. *Melee Weapon Attack:* +7 to hit, reach 5 ft., one target. *Hit:* 5 (1d4 + 3) slashing damage.
Scimitar. *Melee Weapon Attack:* +7 to hit, reach 5 ft., one target. *Hit:* 6 (1d6 + 3) slashing damage.
Hand Crossbow. *Ranged Weapon Attack:* +7 to hit, reach 30/120 ft., one target. *Hit:* 6 (1d6 + 3) piercing damage.

Reactions

Parry. Jall adds 2 to his AC against one melee attack that would hit him. To do so, he must see the attacker and be wielding a melee weapon.
Uncanny Dodge. Jall can halve the damage of an attack against him. To do so, he must see the attacker.

KAMARA B'DU

This tall, striking woman with ebony skin cannot help but have a confident, regal stance, despite her obvious attempts to blend in with the crowd. The armor she wears is accented in white and blue with gold edging and has clearly been perfectly crafted specifically for her. Although she tries to assume a demure attitude, her warm golden brown eyes flash with a confidence and self-assuredness that is unmatched.

Kamara B'du was born during a convergence of environmental anomalies: it was on a night where no stars were seen in the sky, but instead two full moons. And just as dawn broke, a meteor shower began, the shooting stars dissipating at the sun's morning light welcomed in the birth of little Kamara. All her life she heard that she was destined for greatness, to lead the people to the promised land, to bring the waters of life to the barren deserts, to make the world great again like it was in the Age of Heroes. Kamara grew to hate words such as 'prophecy' and 'destiny', wishing only to help those in need. She cared nothing for praise or recognition and knew the only way she would escape from all the attention would be to leave her homeland and travel to a place where no one knew who she was.

While a healer isn't exactly what is needed right now in Cat's Cradle, Kamara still finds herself needed for other divine services, providing knowledge and guidance to any that come for her. Still wishing not to gain any level of notoriety, she rarely works out of any of the popular churches or religious gathering locations, instead opting to work privately in caravan camps or out of taverns and inns. Aside from her expertise in medicines and healing, it is her knowledge in the divine and history that are most often sought after for those looking for guidance.

KAMARA B'DU

Medium humanoid, lawful neutral

Armor Class 17 (scale mail, shield)
Hit Points 29 (5d8 +5)
Speed 30 ft.

STR	DEX	CON	INT	WIS	CHA
10 (+0)	15 (+2)	13 (+1)	12 (+1)	17 (+3)	17 (+3)

Saving Throws Wis +5, Cha +5
Skills History +3, Insight +5, Medicine +5, Persuade +5, Religion +5
Senses passive Perception 13
Languages Celestial, Common, Elvish
Challenge 3 (700 XP)

Disciple of Life. Whenever Kamara uses a spell of 1st level or higher to restore hit points to a creature, the creature regains additional hit points equal to 2 + the spell's level.
Innate spellcasting. Kamara's innate spellcasting ability is Wisdom (spell save DC 16). She can innately cast the following spells, requiring no material components, once per day: *bless, cure wounds, mirror image, pass without trace, beacon of hope, revivify*
Spellcasting. Kamara is a 5th-level spellcaster. Her spellcasting ability is Wisdom (spell save DC 13, +5 to hit with spell attacks). She has the following cleric spells prepared:
Cantrips (at will): *guidance, light, sacred flame, spare the dying*
1st level (4 slots): *bless, cure wounds, detect poison and disease, protection from evil, purify food and drink*
2nd level (3 slots): *lesser restoration, mirror image, pass without trace, silence*
3rd level (2 slots): *beacon of hope, dispel magic, remove curse, revivify*

Actions

Mace. *Melee Weapon Attack:* +2 to hit, reach 5 ft., one target. *Hit:* 3 (1d6) bludgeoning damage.
Crossbow, Light. *Ranged Weapon Attack:* +4 to hit, range 80/320 ft., one target. *Hit:* 6 (1d8 + 2) piercing damage.

Recently struck by a series of dreams with imagery of celestial entities

combatting an unknown darkness, with her as a pivotal figure fighting on the side of light, Kamara has had her opinion of destiny challenged. Because of this, Kamara has reluctantly started a small religious faction dedicated to magic, healing, and shining a cleansing light into the dark corners of the world. Plagued now by the bureaucracy of the city, and the corruption that comes from within, Kamara is in constant need for assistance in protecting not only her temple, but also her followers who ask for aid and guidance when others have turned them away.

KAMARA B'DU
Medium humanoid, lawful neutral

Armor Class 19 (half-plate, shield)
Hit Points 59 (10d8 +10)
Speed 30 ft.

STR	DEX	CON	INT	WIS	CHA
10 (+0)	15 (+2)	13 (+1)	12 (+1)	18 (+4)	18 (+4)

Saving Throws Wis +7, Cha +7
Skills History +4, Insight +7, Medicine +7, Persuade +7, Religion +7
Senses passive Perception 14
Languages Celestial, Common, Elvish
Challenge 6 (2,300 XP)

Blessed Healer. When Kamara casts a spell of 1st level or higher that restores hit points to a creature other than herself, she regains hit points equal to 2 + the spell's level.
Disciple of Life. Whenever Kamara uses a spell of 1st level or higher to restore hit points to a creature, the creature regains additional hit points equal to 2 + the spell's level.
Divine Strike. Once per turn, when Kamara hits a creature with a weapon attack, she can cause the attack to deal an additional 1d8 radiant damage to the target.
Innate spellcasting. Kamara's innate spellcasting ability is Wisdom (spell save DC 16). She can innately cast the following spells, requiring no material components, once per day: *bless,*

cure wounds, mirror image, pass without trace, beacon of hope, revivify, death ward, guardian of faith, mass cure wounds, raise dead.
Spellcasting. Kamara is a 10th-level spellcaster. Her spellcasting ability is Wisdom (spell save DC 15, +7 to hit with spell attacks). She has the following cleric spells prepared:
Cantrips (at will): *guidance, light, sacred flame, spare the dying*
1st level (4 slots): *bless, cure wounds, detect poison and disease, protection from evil, purify food and drink*
2nd level (3 slots): *lesser restoration, mirror image, pass without trace, silence*
3rd level (3 slots): *beacon of hope, dispel magic, remove curse, revivify, speak with dead*
4th level (3 slots): *banishment, death ward, freedom of movement, guardian of faith*
5th level (2 slots): *commune, mass cure wounds, raise dead*

Actions

Mace. *Melee Weapon Attack:* +3 to hit, reach 5 ft., one target. *Hit:* 3 (1d6) bludgeoning damage.
Crossbow, Light. *Ranged Weapon Attack:* +5 to hit, range 80/320 ft., one target. *Hit:* 6 (1d8 + 2) piercing damage.

After all these years, Kamara B'du has decided to begin embracing her destiny. After a powerful encounter with a Deva named Zephiriel, the hidden potential within her was tapped and Kamara's celestial heritage blossomed. She is still coming to grips with what that means about her dreams and visions, but her confidence in herself and her new path are clear. She hopes to get a message back to her family and let them all know what has happened, with her returning to them one day.

Kamara's order, now calling themselves the Guardians of the Light, have around thirty primary members and double that in acolytes. The ranked regular primaries consist of clerics, paladins, fighters, and alchemists dedicated to helping those in need, seeking the truth in all things, and fighting evil whenever they can. While services are held every dawn by her cleric underlings, Kamara only leads sermons for special occasions, holidays, and the evenings of a full moon.

The Guardians of Light have grown too big for their previous headquarters and are seeking a larger locale. They will pay players a "finder's fee" for information on a suitable location (either within the city of Cat's Cradle or in the surrounding land) that they can relocate to.

KAMARA B'DU, BEARER OF THE LIGHT
Medium celestial, lawful neutral

Armor Class 21 (+1 gleaming half-plate, +1 shield)
Hit Points 127 (15d8 + 60)
Speed 30 ft., fly 60 ft.

STR	DEX	CON	INT	WIS	CHA
10 (+0)	15 (+2)	18 (+4)	12 (+1)	20 (+5)	20 (+5)

Saving Throws Wis +9, Cha +9
Skills History +5, Insight +9, Medicine +9, Persuade +9, Religion +9
Damage Resistances radiant; bludgeoning, piercing, and slashing attacks from nonmagical attacks
Condition Immunities charmed, exhaustion, frightened
Senses darkvision 120 ft., passive Perception 15
Languages Celestial, Common, Elvish
Challenge 10 (5,900 XP)

Angelic Weapons. Kamara's weapon attacks are magical. When she hits with any weapon, the weapon deals an extra 4d8 radiant damage (included in the attack)
Blessed Healer. When Kamara casts a spell of 1st level or higher that restores hit points to a creature other than herself, she regains hit points equal to 2 + the spell's level.
Disciple of Life. Whenever Kamara uses a spell of 1st level or higher to restore hit points to a creature, the creature regains additional hit points equal to 2 + the spell's level.
Magic Resistance. Kamara has advantage on saving throws against spells and other magical effects.

Innate spellcasting. Kamara's innate spellcasting ability is Wisdom (spell save DC 16). She can innately cast the following spells, requiring no material components, once per day: *bless, cure wounds, mirror image, pass without trace, beacon of hope, revivify, death ward, guardian of faith, mass cure wounds, raise dead.*

Spellcasting. Kamara is a 15th-level spellcaster. Her spellcasting ability is Wisdom (spell save DC 17, +9 to hit with spell attacks). She has the following cleric spells prepared:

Cantrips (at will): *guidance, light, sacred flame, spare the dying*

1st level (4 slots): *bless, cure wounds, detect poison and disease, protection from evil, purify food and drink*

2nd level (3 slots): *lesser restoration, prayer of healing, spiritual weapon, zone of truth*

3rd level (3 slots): *beacon of hope, dispel magic, remove curse, revivify, speak with dead*

4th level (3 slots): *banishment, death ward, freedom of movement, guardian of faith*

5th level (2 slots): *commune, mass cure wounds, raise dead*

6th level (1 slots): *heal*

7th level (1 slots): *conjure celestial*

8th level (1 slots): *holy aura*

Actions

Multiattack. Kamara makes two melee attacks.

Mace. Melee Weapon Attack: +4 to hit, reach 5 ft., one target. *Hit:* 3 (1d6) bludgeoning damage plus 18 (4d8) radiant damage.

Crossbow, Light. Ranged Weapon Attack: +6 to hit, range 80/320 ft., one target. *Hit:* 6 (1d8 + 2) piercing damage plus 18 (4d8) radiant damage.

MATTEA THEASEAN

Young and devoted to keeping order in Cat's Cradle, Mattea Theasean joined the City Watch several years ago, quickly rising through the ranks while growing disillusioned with the organization's corruption and lax attitude toward law enforcement. When she was involved in tracking down the Dockside Lurker, a ruthless robber and murderer who plagued the waterfront, Mattea gained the notice of Lady Genera, the tough and wizened commander of the Constabulary and was recruited into the organization. Mattea immediately distinguished herself, and when uprooting a smuggling operation by the Kennock Syndicate, proved to be utterly incorruptible. In the process she made several prominent enemies, but continued to perform her duty, completely undeterred.

Over the years, Mattea has studied both arcane and divine magic, applying it to her career as an investigator. She cuts a dramatic figure, clad in her long leather coat, armed with both rapier and a hand crossbow with poisoned bolts. Her spellcasting abilities and her choice of weapons has led some to suggest that she has some history with the drow, or may indeed have dark elf ancestors, but Matter herself is quite secretive about her past.

MATTEA THEASEAN

Medium humanoid (elf), lawful neutral

Armor Class 13 (leather armor)
Hit Points 72 (16d8)
Speed 30 ft.

STR	DEX	CON	INT	WIS	CHA
10 (+0)	14 (+2)	10 (+0)	16 (+3)	14 (+2)	16 (+3)

Saving Throws Dex +4, Wis +4
Skills Acrobatics +4, Deception +5, History +5, Insight +4, Intimidation +5, Investigation +5, Perception +4, Persuasion +5, Sleight of Hand +4, Stealth +4
Senses darkvision 60 ft., passive Perception 14
Languages Common, Dwarvish, Elvish, Sylvan
Challenge 3 (700 XP)

Fey Ancestry. Mattea Theasean has advantage on saving throws against being charmed, and magic can't put her to sleep.

Arcane Spellcasting. Mattea Theasean is a 3rd-level spellcaster.

Her spellcasting ability is Charisma (spell save DC 13, +5 to hit with spell attacks). She has the following sorcerer spells prepared:

Cantrips (at will): *dancing lights, friends, mage hand, shocking grasp*

1st level (4 slots): *charm person, comprehend languages*

2nd level (2 slots): *alter self, detect thoughts*

Divine Spellcasting. Mattea Theasean is a 3rd-level spellcaster. Her spellcasting ability is Wisdom (spell save DC 12, +4 to hit with spell attacks). She has the following cleric spells prepared:

Cantrips (at will): *guidance, spare the dying, thaumaturgy*

1st level (4 slots): *command, cure wounds, detect evil and good, sanctuary*

2nd level (3 slots): *locate object, zone of truth,*

Investigator. Mattea Theasean has advantage on Dexterity (Stealth) and Wisdom (Perception) checks.

Sneak Attack. Once per turn, Mattea can deal an extra 7 (2d6) damage to one creature she hits with a Rapier attack if she has advantage on the attack roll. She does not need advantage on the attack roll if another enemy of the target is within 5 feet of her, that enemy isn't incapacitated, and she does not disadvantage on the attack roll.

Actions

Rapier. Melee Weapon Attack: +4 to hit, reach 5 ft., one target. *Hit:* 6 (1d8 + 2) piercing damage.

Hand Crossbow. Ranged Weapon Attack: +4 to hit, range 30/120 ft., one target. *Hit:* 5 (1d6 + 2) piercing damage and the target must succeed on a DC 13 Constitution saving throw or be poisoned for 1 hour. If the saving throw fails by 5 or more, the target is also unconscious while poisoned in this way. The target wakes up if it takes damage or if another creature takes an action to shake them awake.

Despite years on the street and continued exposure to even more corruption and crime, Mattea has grown more compassionate toward victims and has even begun to develop a certain understanding and empathy for some criminals, seeing that some folk are forced into lives of illegal activities by circumstances beyond their control. One sign of her evolving nature is her professional alliance with private investigator Valdrin Hoff, an individual known for both his hatred of crime that victimizes the weak, and his tendency to mete out justice on his own terms. Though she feels some distaste for Hoff's occasional vigilantism, she nevertheless continues to share information with him. She has kept their relationship quiet, especially around her superiors.

She carries a scar on her face from a Syndicate assassin, and she refuses any arcane healing or cosmetic surgery. A grateful artificer enchanted her signature leather coat, granting it a +1 bonus to AC, and she carries the unique *Investigator's Staff* and is accompanied by her **raven** familiar, Kaen (with Intelligence 6 and Wisdom 16).

MATTEA THEASEAN
Medium humanoid (elf), lawful good

Armor Class 14 (*leather armor of protection*)
Hit Points 90 (20d8)
Speed 30 ft.

STR	DEX	CON	INT	WIS	CHA
10 (+0)	14 (+2)	10 (+0)	16 (+3)	16 (+3)	16 (+3)

Saving Throws Dex +5, Wis +6
Skills Acrobatics +5, Deception +6, History +6, Insight +6, Intimidation +6, Investigation +6, Perception +6, Persuasion +6, Sleight of Hand +5, Stealth +5
Senses darkvision 60 ft., passive Perception 16
Languages Common, Dwarvish, Elvish, Sylvan
Challenge 6 (2300 XP)

Fey Ancestry. Mattea Theasean has advantage on saving throws against being charmed, and magic can't put her to sleep.
Arcane Spellcasting. Mattea Theasean is a 4th-level spellcaster. Her spellcasting ability is Charisma (spell save DC 14, +6 to hit with spell attacks). She has the following sorcerer spells prepared:
Cantrips (at will): *dancing lights, friends, mage hand, shocking grasp*
1st level (4 slots): *charm person, comprehend languages, silent image*
2nd level (3 slots): *alter self, detect thoughts*
Divine Spellcasting. Mattea Theasean is a 4th-level spellcaster. Her spellcasting ability is Wisdom (spell save DC 14, +6 to hit with spell attacks). She has the following cleric spells prepared:
Cantrips (at will): *guidance, light, sacred flame, thaumaturgy*
1st level (4 slots): *command, cure wounds, sanctuary*
2nd level (3 slots): *hold person, zone of truth*
Investigator. Mattea Theasean has advantage on Dexterity (Stealth) and Wisdom (Perception) checks.
Investigator's Staff. Mattea has advantage on Charisma (Persuasion), Intelligence (Investigation), and Wisdom (Insight) checks. She can also use the staff to cast certain spells. See side box for details.
Sneak Attack. Once per turn, Mattea can deal an extra 10 (3d6) damage to one creature she hits with a Rapier attack if she has advantage on the attack roll. She does not need advantage on the attack roll if another enemy of the target is within 5 feet of her, that enemy isn't incapacitated, and she does not disadvantage on the attack roll.
Uncanny Dodge. When an attacker that Mattea can see see hits her with an attack, she can use her reaction to halve the attack's damage against her.

Actions

Investigator's Staff. *Melee Weapon Attack:* +4 to hit, reach 5 ft., one target. *Hit:* 4 (1d6 + 1) bludgeoning damage or 5 (1d8 + 1) bludgeoning damage if used with two hands.
Rapier. *Melee Weapon Attack:* +5 to hit, reach 5 ft., one target. *Hit:* 7 (1d8 + 3) piercing damage.
Hand Crossbow. *Ranged Weapon Attack:* +5 to hit, range 30/120 ft., one target. *Hit:* 6 (1d6 + 3) piercing damage and the target

INVESTIGATOR'S STAFF
Weapon (staff), very rare (requires attunement)

This item functions as a *quarterstaff +1*, and while carrying it you gain advantage on Charisma (Persuasion), Intelligence (Investigation), and Wisdom (Insight) checks.

The *investigator's staff* has 10 charges. While holding it, you can use an action to expend one or more charges to cast one of the following spells, using your spell save DC and spellcasting ability modifier: *light* (0 charges), *detect magic* (1 charge), *sleep* (1 charge), *invisibility* (2 charges), *see invisibility* (2 charges), *clairvoyance* (3 charges), *locate object* (3 charges), *nondetection* (3 charges), *arcane eye* (4 charges), *scrying* (5 charges). The staff regains 1d6 + 4 charges each day at dawn.

must succeed on a DC 13 Constitution saving throw or be poisoned for 1 hour. If the saving throw fails by 5 or more, the target is also unconscious while poisoned in this way. The target wakes up if it takes damage or if another creature takes an action to shake them awake.

Now a senior investigator and thought by many to one day be destined for the office of Chief Constable, Mattea Theasen has grown into a far more compassionate and pragmatic individual than she was earlier in her career. Though she is scarred, tough, and uncompromising in her pursuit of criminals, she has learned much about forgiveness and understanding. While others who enforce the law may have become more cynical and grim-hearted, Theasen appears to have gone in the other direction, and today is a dedicated defender of the weak and the downtrodden, willing to overlook or lend help to those whom circumstances force into illegal acts. Crime bosses, killers, career criminals and others should not rely on her merciful streak however, for she also knows the difference between the unlucky, the ignorant and the truly evil. She continues to wield her trusty *investigator's staff* and a *+2 rapier*, a gift from her grateful fellow Constables. Her raven now has an Intelligence score of 8 and can both speak and understand Common.

MATTEA THEASEAN
Medium humanoid (elf), neutral good

Armor Class 14 (*leather armor of protection*)
Hit Points 135 (30d8)
Speed 30 ft.

STR	DEX	CON	INT	WIS	CHA
10 (+0)	14 (+2)	10 (+0)	18 (+4)	16 (+3)	16 (+3)

Saving Throws Dex +5, Wis +6
Skills Acrobatics +6, Deception +7, History +8, Insight +7, Intimidation +7, Investigation +8, Perception +7, Persuasion +7, Sleight of Hand +6, Stealth +6
Senses darkvision 60 ft., passive Perception 17
Languages Common, Dwarvish, Elvish, Sylvan
Challenge 10 (5900 XP)

Fey Ancestry. Mattea Theasean has advantage on saving throws against being charmed, and magic can't put her to sleep.
Arcane Spellcasting. Mattea Theasean is a 6th-level spellcaster. Her spellcasting ability is Charisma (spell save DC 15, +7 to hit with spell attacks). She has the following sorcerer spells prepared:
Cantrips (at will): *dancing lights, friends, mage hand, shocking grasp*
1st level (4 slots): *charm person, comprehend languages, silent image*
2nd level (3 slots): *alter self, detect thoughts*
3rd level (3 slots): *daylight, tongues*
Divine Spellcasting. Mattea Theasean is a 6th-level spellcaster. Her spellcasting ability is Wisdom (spell save DC 15, +7 to hit with spell attacks). She has the following cleric spells prepared:
Cantrips (at will): *guidance, light, sacred flame, thaumaturgy*
1st level (4 slots): *command, cure wounds, detect evil and good,*

sanctuary
2nd level (3 slots): *hold person, locate object, zone of truth*
3rd level (3 slots): *dispel magic, remove curse, speak with dead*

Investigator. Mattea Theasean has advantage on Dexterity (Stealth) and Wisdom (Perception) checks.

Investigator's Staff. Mattea has advantage on Charisma (Persuasion), Intelligence (Investigation), and Wisdom (Insight) checks. She can also use the staff to cast certain spells. See side box for details.

Sneak Attack. Once per turn, Mattea can deal an extra 13 (4d6) damage to one creature she hits with a Rapier attack if she has advantage on the attack roll. She does not need advantage on the attack roll if another enemy of the target is within 5 feet of her, that enemy isn't incapacitated, and she does not disadvantage on the attack roll.

Uncanny Dodge. When an attacker that Mattea can see see hits her with an attack, she can use her reaction to halve the attack's damage against her.

Evasion. If subjected to an effect that allows her to make a Dexterity saving throw to take only half damage, she instead takes no damage if she succeeds on the saving throw, and only half damage if she fails.

Actions

Investigator's Staff. *Melee Weapon Attack:* +5 to hit, reach 5 ft., one target. *Hit:* 4(1d6 + 1) bludgeoning damage or 5 (1d8 + 1) bludgeoning damage if used with two hands.

+2 Rapier. *Melee Weapon Attack:* +8 to hit, reach 5 ft., one target. *Hit:* 8 (1d8 + 4) piercing damage.

Hand Crossbow. *Ranged Weapon Attack:* +6 to hit, range 30/120 ft., one target. *Hit:* 5 (1d6 + 2) piercing damage and the target must succeed on a DC 13 Constitution saving throw or be poisoned for 1 hour. If the saving throw fails by 5 or more, the target is also unconscious while poisoned in this way. The target wakes up if it takes damage or if another creature takes an action to shake them awake.

MINTRA KOHLER

A very pale woman stands unassumingly off to one side, quietly watching her surroundings. While tall and lanky, she is clearly fit and athletic. She wears a loosely fitting pair of dark pants and a black and white pulled hair up high on the back of her head, held in place by two ornately carved hairpins. She carries a simple drawstring bag on her back and leans against a long quarterstaff made of blackened ironwood. But it is her cold, emotionless black eyes, when she turns her attention to you, that are the most off-putting, especially since her expressionless face does nothing to ease the unnerving tension caused by her stare.

When Mintra was just a girl, growing up in the Skyforge of the Blue Soul monastery far to the East, she was part of a small group of youths that experienced a deadly malady. This sickness caused them all to fall into a deep sleep and the blood in their veins to harden, almost as hard as stone. Half of the young ones died as a result, but those that recovered and awakened spoke of a shadowy, fog-filled wood and a dark voice calling out to them. As the years passed, each of the children that had been affected by the "Stone Blood Curse" had their memories of the incident washed away, suppressed deep into the recesses of their mind… but not Mintra. Every night since she reawakened, she dreamed of that voice in the dark forest calling out to her, and while it frightened her, she felt drawn to it and compelled to seek it out. When Mintra came of age, she left the monastery to search for answers and to gain knowledge of how to fill the hole she felt in her soul.

MINTRA KOHLER

Medium humanoid, lawful neutral

Armor Class 16 (unarmored defense)
Hit Points 52 (8d8 + 16)
Speed 40 ft.

STR	DEX	CON	INT	WIS	CHA
14 (+2)	17 (+3)	15 (+2)	11 (+0)	16 (+3)	11 (+0)

Saving Throws Str +4, Dex +5
Skills Acrobatics +5, History +2, Religion +2
Senses passive Perception 13
Languages Common
Challenge 3 (700 XP)

Innate Spellcasting. Mintra's spellcasting ability is Wisdom (spell save DC 13). Once per day she may cast the following spells without material components: *darkness, darkvision, minor illusion, pass without trace, silence.*

Ki Strikes. Mintra's unarmed strikes count as magical for purposes of overcoming resistance and immunity to nonmagical attacks and damage.

Stunning Blows (1/turn). When Mintra hits another creature with a melee attack, that creature must succeed on a DC 13 Constitution saving throw or be stunned until the end of Mintra's next turn.

Actions

Multiattack. Mintra makes four Unarmed Strikes or two ranged attacks.

Unarmed Strike. *Melee Weapon Attack:* +5 to hit, reach 5 ft., one target. *Hit:* 5 (1d4 + 3) bludgeoning damage.

Light Crossbow. *Ranged Weapon Attack:* +5 to hit, range 80/320 ft., one target. *Hit:* 7 (1d8 + 3) piercing damage

Still new to the Cat's Cradle region, Mintra the monk has struggled to find her place. A region of progress, with its bustling commerce and daily turnaround of travelers, both to and from the city itself, she quickly realized that the answers she was seeking would not come easily. But she knows she is in the right place, for the world seems more in focus for her than ever since leaving the Skyforge of the Blue Soul monastery. Not only that, but the voice from her dreams is now clearer than ever before, its dark song filling her with purpose and calling to her from the wilderness beyond the city walls. Not from the lakes, not the hills and salt mines, but from the forest, the power has been pulling at her mind. In addition, a name has come to her that she cannot shake: The Shrouded Ruins of Atenam. Whether this name came to her in her sleep, or if she gleaned it off a strange wayfaring traveler, she cannot say, but as soon as she heard it, it was as if a gong had been struck within her heart and her head. She knew that if she found this place, her questions would finally be answered.

MINTRA KOHLER
Medium humanoid, lawful neutral

Armor Class 17 (unarmored defense)
Hit Points 78 (12d8 + 24)
Speed 45 ft.

STR	DEX	CON	INT	WIS	CHA
14 (+2)	18 (+4)	15 (+2)	11 (+0)	16 (+3)	11 (+0)

Saving Throws Str +5, Dex +7
Skills Acrobatics +7, History +3, Religion +3
Condition Immunities charmed, frightened
Senses passive Perception 13
Languages Common
Challenge 6 (2,300 XP)

Evasion. If Mintra is subjected to an effect that allows her to make a Dexterity saving throw to take only half damage, Mintra instead takes no damage if she succeeds on the saving throw, and only half damage if she fails.

Innate Spellcasting. Mintra's spellcasting ability is Wisdom (spell save DC 13). Once per day she may cast the following spells without material components: *darkness, darkvision, minor illusion, pass without trace, silence.*

Ki Strikes. Mintra's unarmed strikes count as magical for purposes of overcoming resistance and immunity to nonmagical attacks and damage.

Shadow Step. When Mintra is in dim light or darkness, as a bonus action she can teleport up to 60 feet to an unoccupied space she can see that is also in dim light or darkness. She then has advantage on the first melee attack she takes before the end of the turn.

Stunning Blows (1/turn). When Mintra hits another creature with a melee attack, that creature must succeed on a DC 14 Constitution saving throw or be stunned until the end of Mintra's next turn.

Actions

Multiattack. Mintra makes four Unarmed Strikes or two ranged attacks.

Unarmed Strike. *Melee Weapon Attack:* +6 to hit, reach 5 ft., one target. *Hit:* 6 (1d6 + 3) bludgeoning damage.

Light Crossbow. *Ranged Weapon Attack:* +6 to hit, range 80/320 ft., one target. *Hit:* 7 (1d8 + 3) piercing damage

Mintra the Unburnt is the guardian of the hidden Atenam Grove in the Cantricle Forest, acting as a bodyguard and scout, but also as a thug enforcer and kidnapper for her new masters. Freshly imbued with a fiendish blessing by an Archdruid of the Order of the Old Oak, for loyalty and services rendered, she has started down the path to become one with the entity that reached out to her all those years ago. While Mintra herself is not a cleric or druid, she has used the energies granted to her to finely hone her martial prowess and to further perfect her body and mind. Often roaming the streets of Cat's Cradle, or frequenting popular taverns within the city, she likes to keep tabs on newcomers into the area, or for potential marks she can knock out and take back to the druids of the wood. While she is more than capable of handling herself in a fight, she always has a small squad of young druid acolytes and cutthroats with her, awaiting her signal. Recently, Mintra has been laying low as she recently kidnapped the daughter of a local noble, Willowren Skystar, and smuggled her into the forest.

MINTRA KOHLER
Medium humanoid, lawful evil

Armor Class 18 (unarmored defense)
Hit Points 120 (16d8 + 48)
Speed 50 ft.

STR	DEX	CON	INT	WIS	CHA
14 (+2)	18 (+4)	16 (+3)	11 (+0)	18 (+4)	11 (+0)

Saving Throws Str +6, Dex +8
Skills Acrobatics +8, History +4, Religion +4, Stealth +8
Damage Immunities fire
Condition Immunities charmed, disease, frightened, poisoned
Senses passive Perception 14
Languages All
Challenge 10 (5,900 XP)

Blessing of the Old Oak. When a creature makes an attack against Mintra and misses, she has advantage on the first melee attack she takes against that creature before the end of her next turn.

Evasion. If Mintra is subjected to an effect that allows her to make a Dexterity saving throw to take only half damage, Mintra instead takes no damage if she succeeds on the saving throw, and only half damage if she fails.

Innate Spellcasting. Mintra's spellcasting ability is Wisdom (spell save DC 13). Once per day she may cast the following spells without material components: *darkness, darkvision, minor illusion, pass without trace, silence.*

Ki Strikes. Mintra's unarmed strikes count as magical for purposes of overcoming resistance and immunity to nonmagical attacks and damage.

Shadow Step. When Mintra is in dim light or darkness, as a bonus action she can teleport up to 60 feet to an unoccupied space she can see that is also in dim light or darkness. She then has advantage on the first melee attack she takes before the end of the turn.

Stunning Blows (1/turn). When Mintra hits another creature with a melee attack, that creature must succeed on a Constitution saving throw against DC 15 or be stunned until the end of Mintra's next turn.

Actions

Multiattack. Mintra makes four Unarmed Strikes or two ranged attacks.

Unarmed Strike. *Melee Weapon Attack:* +7 to hit, reach 5 ft., one target. *Hit:* 8 (1d8 + 4) bludgeoning damage, plus 3 (1d6) fire damage.

Light Crossbow. *Ranged Weapon Attack:* +7 to hit, range 80/320 ft., one target. *Hit:* 8 (1d8 + 4) piercing damage

Cloak of Shadows. When Mintra is in dim light or darkness, she may become invisible. She remains invisible until she attacks or is in an area of bright light.

OJA KORBIS

This nimble half-elven woman smirks at you from the rafters before falling backward into a double somersault and landing effortlessly on her feet. Wearing leather armor, loose attire, and a belt of knives around her waist, this olive-skinned woman ties a blue sash around her head to keep her flowing black hair out of her eyes before giving another sly smile. "Wotcher!" She flips a pair of daggers out of their sheaths, inspects the blades, then returns them with a spinning flourish.

An orphan and runaway, Oja has always been tough and independent, but in spite of the hardships of her youth, she has never let her positive attitude be diminished. Able to make friends wherever she has traveled, Oja is bold and outgoing, and never backs down from opposition. As she tends to have an affinity with the downtrodden, poor, and "the little guy", Oja has been known to partake in heists or jobs against wealthy targets so that she can then turn around and generously give back to those in need.

Although she has only been in Cat's Cradle a short while, Oja has quickly learned whom to trust and whom to avoid in town, and can serve as a guide for other newcomers. She helps gather information for Jall Kukrich, has a passing friendship with Valdrin Hoff, and is an acquaintance with Garron Thorn (whose business she respectfully keeps out of, despite having "acquired" a few items for him when she first arrived in town).

OJA KORBIS, THE BLUE FOX

Medium humanoid, chaotic good

Armor Class 14 (leather)
Hit Points 44 (8d8 + 8)
Speed 30 ft.

STR	DEX	CON	INT	WIS	CHA
12 (+1)	17 (+3)	13 (+1)	15 (+2)	17 (+3)	15 (+2)

Saving Throws Dex +5, Cha +4
Skills Acrobatics +7, Arcana +4, Deception +4, Insight +5, Perception +5, Persuasion +4, Sleight of Hand +7, Stealth +5
Senses passive Perception 15
Languages Common, Dwarvish, Elvish, Gnomish, Orcish
Challenge 3 (700 XP)

Cunning Action. On each of her turns, Oja can use a bonus action to take the Dash, Disengage, or Hide action.

Sneak Attack (1/turn). Oja deals an extra 7 (2d6) damage when she hits a target with a weapon attack and has advantage on the attack roll, or when the target is within 5 feet of an ally of theirs that isn't incapacitated and Oja doesn't have disadvantage on the attack roll.

Spellcasting. Oja is a 2nd-level spellcaster. Her spellcasting ability is Wisdom (spell save DC 13, +5 to hit with spell attacks). She has the following cleric spells prepared:
Cantrips (at will): *guidance, mending, sacred flame*
1st level (3 slots): *command, detect magic, identify, sanctuary*

Actions

Dagger. *Melee or Ranged Weapon Attack:* +5 to hit, reach 5 ft. or range 20/60 ft., one target. *Hit:* 5 (1d4 + 3) piercing damage.
Rapier. *Melee Weapon Attack:* +5 to hit, reach 5 ft., one target. *Hit:* 6 (1d6 + 3) piercing damage.
Shortbow. *Ranged Weapon Attack:* +5 to hit, reach 80/320 ft., one target. *Hit:* 6 (1d6 + 3) piercing damage.

Whip. *Melee Weapon Attack:* +5 to hit, reach 10 ft., one target. *Hit:* 5 (1d4 + 3) slashing damage

Oja Korbis, under the guise of the masked vigilante known as the Blue Fox, has made a name for herself by stealing from the rich and powerful to provide support for the orphanages, street urchins, and other poor folk in Cat's Cradle and surrounding locales. While "on the job" she tends to work alone, Oja still maintains her contacts with the other prominent information brokers and thieves in town as well as making sure not to step on any toes. She has a more strained relationship with the authorities of town, as her activities have gotten more and more illegal of late.

Through her various heists, Oja has begun to hone her knowledges and has become a bit of an amateur historian when it comes to pieces of art, rare components, and magic items. She usually fences her items through Jall Kukrich, although lately she has been acquiring some otherworldly pieces of art that she has decided to keep to herself to investigate more. Should any players wish to assist her in her investigations, or should they come across any such items themselves, Oja will offer compensation for them.

OJA KORBIS, THE BLUE FOX

Medium humanoid, chaotic good

Armor Class 15 (studded leather)
Hit Points 66 (12d8 + 12)
Speed 30 ft.

STR	DEX	CON	INT	WIS	CHA
12 (+1)	18 (+4)	13 (+1)	15 (+2)	17 (+3)	15 (+2)

Saving Throws Dex +7, Cha +5
Skills Acrobatics +10, Arcana +5, Deception +5, History +5, Insight +6, Perception +6, Persuasion +5, Sleight of Hand +10, Stealth +7
Senses passive Perception 16
Languages Common, Dwarvish, Elvish, Gnomish, Orcish
Challenge 6 (2,300 XP)

Cunning Action. On each of her turns, Oja can use a bonus action to take the Dash, Disengage, Hide or Use an Object action.

Sneak Attack (1/turn). Oja deals an extra 10 (3d6) damage when she hits a target with a weapon attack and has advantage on the attack roll, or when the target is within 5 feet of an ally of theirs that isn't incapacitated and Oja doesn't have disadvantage on the attack roll.

Spellcasting. Oja is a 4th-level spellcaster. Her spellcasting ability is Wisdom (spell save DC 14, +6 to hit with spell attacks). She has the following cleric spells prepared:
Cantrips (at will): *guidance, mending, sacred flame, thaumaturgy*
1st level (4 slots): *command, detect magic, identify, protection from evil, sanctuary*
2nd level (3 slots): *augur, hold person, protection from poison, suggestion*

Actions

Dagger. *Melee or Ranged Weapon Attack:* +7 to hit, reach 5 ft. or range 20/60 ft., one target. *Hit:* 6 (1d4 + 4) piercing damage.
Rapier. *Melee Weapon Attack:* +7 to hit, reach 5 ft., one target. *Hit:* 7 (1d6 + 4) piercing damage.
Shortbow. *Ranged Weapon Attack:* +7 to hit, reach 80/320 ft., one target. *Hit:* 7 (1d6 + 4) piercing damage.
Whip. *Melee Weapon Attack:* +7 to hit, reach 10 ft., one target. *Hit:* 6 (1d4 + 4) slashing damage

Reactions

Uncanny Dodge. Oja can halve the damage of an attack against her. To do so, she must see the attacker.

Oja Korbis has recently broken her way out of the Cat's Cradle jail with the help of a handful of orphans and street urchins and is on the lam. Luckily, her persona as the Blue Fox was not compromised, so she is able to operate in disguise as she investigates who betrayed her and framed her for the murder of an alchemist within the city limits (a halfling fellow by the name of Adric Waterhouse). Oja suspects her framing has something to do with the mysterious statuettes and trinkets she has been finding circulating around town. These items give her a growing concern that there is a gathering of a dark organization or guild that is starting to operate in the area. Does this have something to do with the mining and salts of the region? Or is there something more sinister afoot? The Blue Fox does not know but hopes that she can uncover what is really happening.

OJA KORBIS
Medium humanoid, chaotic good

Armor Class 16 (chain shirt)
Hit Points 88 (16d8 + 16)
Speed 30 ft.

STR	DEX	CON	INT	WIS	CHA
12 (+1)	20 (+5)	13 (+1)	15 (+2)	18 (+4)	15 (+2)

Saving Throws Dex +9, Cha +6
Skills Acrobatics +13, Arcana +10, Deception +6, History +10, Insight +8, Perception +8, Persuasion +6, Sleight of Hand +13, Stealth +9
Senses passive Perception 18
Languages Common, Dwarvish, Elvish, Gnomish, Orcish
Challenge 10 (5,900 XP)

Cunning Action. On each of her turns, Oja can use a bonus action to take the Dash, Disengage, Hide or Use an Object action.
Evasion. If Oja is subjected to an effect that allows her to make a Dexterity saving throw to take only half damage, Oja instead takes no damage if she succeeds on the saving throw, and only half damage if she fails.
Sneak Attack (1/turn). Oja deals an extra 14 (4d6) damage when she hits a target with a weapon attack and has advantage on the attack roll, or when the target is within 5 feet of an ally of theirs that isn't incapacitated and Oja doesn't have disadvantage on the attack roll.
Spellcasting. Oja is a 6th-level spellcaster. Her spellcasting ability is Wisdom (spell save DC 16, +8 to hit with spell attacks). She has the following cleric spells prepared:
Cantrips (at will): *guidance, mending, sacred flame, thaumaturgy*
1st level (4 slots): *command, detect magic, identify, protection from evil, sanctuary*
2nd level (3 slots): *augury, hold person, protection from poison, suggestion*
3rd level (3 slots): *dispel magic, feign death, nondetection, speak with dead*

Actions

Dagger. *Melee or Ranged Weapon Attack:* +9 to hit, reach 5 ft. or range 20/60 ft., one target. *Hit:* 7 (1d4 + 5) piercing damage.
Rapier. *Melee Weapon Attack:* +9 to hit, reach 5 ft., one target. *Hit:* 8 (1d6 + 5) piercing damage.
Shortbow. *Ranged Weapon Attack:* +9 to hit, reach 80/320 ft., one target. *Hit:* 8 (1d6 + 5) piercing damage.
Whip. *Melee Weapon Attack:* +9 to hit, reach 10 ft., one target. *Hit:* 7 (1d4 + 5) slashing damage

Reactions

Uncanny Dodge. Oja can halve the damage of an attack against her. To do so, she must see the attacker.

THE RAVEN

   The rogue simply known as *"the Raven"* lurks silently in the shadows, almost becoming one with the darkness. They wear a plague doctor style black leather mask to obscure their facial features. Their lithe, muscular form is dressed in masterfully crafted black and silver leather armor, and they are wearing a wide brim hat and cloak. Adorned with countless throwing blades, they also use a rapier and scimitar in melee combat, and a longbow and quiver of black-fletched arrows can also be seen hanging off their back.

   This leather-clad elf with the blonde and pink hair and a scarred face typically keeps to themself in the corner of the tavern, drinking their bitter tea and munching on dried fruit. If offered food or drink more delicious than what they are currently imbibing, the Raven declines in a quiet voice, just above a whisper, stating that they don't have a taste for such things. In any case, the lithe rogue doesn't balk at company, nor overtly shy away from direct conversation, despite looking uncomfortable at direct contact with people. Originally from the town of Dancer to the, the Raven not only came to Cat's Cradle looking for work, but also to find a couple of cousins of theirs that came to the region and then went missing.

THE RAVEN
Medium humanoid, lawful neutral

Armor Class 15 (leather)
Hit Points 36 (8d8 + 8)
Speed 30 ft.

STR	DEX	CON	INT	WIS	CHA
12 (+1)	17 (+3)	13 (+1)	14 (+2)	15 (+2)	13 (+1)

Saving Throws Dex +5, Int +4
Skills Arcana +4, Acrobatics +7, Perception +4, Sleight of Hand +5, Stealth +7
Condition Immunities charmed, disease, frightened, poison
Senses passive Perception 14

Languages Common, Dwarvish, Elvish
Challenge 3 (700 XP)

Assassinate. The Raven has advantage on attack rolls against any creature that hasn't taken a turn in the combat yet. In addition, any hit the Raven scores against a creature that is surprised is a critical hit.

Evasion. If the Raven is subjected to an effect that allows them to make a Dexterity saving throw to take only half damage, the Raven instead takes no damage if they succeed on the saving throw, and only half damage if they fail.

Sneak Attack (1/turn). The Raven deals an extra 7 (2d6) damage when they hit a target with a weapon attack and has advantage on the attack roll, or when the target is within 5 feet of an ally of theirs that isn't incapacitated, and the Raven doesn't have disadvantage on the attack roll.

Actions

Multiattack. The Raven makes two melee attacks.
Scimitar. *Melee Weapon Attack:* +5 to hit, reach 5 ft., one target. *Hit:* 6 (1d6 + 3) slashing damage.
Rapier. *Melee Weapon Attack:* +5 to hit, reach 5 ft., one target. *Hit:* 7 (1d8 + 3) piercing damage.
Dagger. *Melee or Ranged Weapon Attack:* +5 to hit, reach 5 ft. or range 20/60 ft., one target. *Hit:* 5 (1d4 + 3) piercing damage
Longbow. *Ranged Weapon Attack:* +5 to hit, range 150/600 ft., one target. *Hit:* 7 (1d8 + 3) piercing damage

Reactions

Uncanny Dodge. The Raven can halve the damage of an attack against them. To do so, they must see the attacker.

Since they received their answers as to the fate of their lost kin, the Raven has become a full-fledged mercenary-for-hire within the city and surrounding areas of Cat's Cradle. Almost exclusively wearing the trademark plague doctor mask wherever they go, the Raven has earned the reputation of someone who gets the job done. Whatever skills are lacking are overshadowed by the pure determination the Raven exhibits in ensuring a job get done. While typically any job is open for them, there is still a code that is followed: no robbing or harming the poor and destitute, and no killing of innocents. While it cannot be proved, it is rumored that certain members of the city guard have taken to unofficially hiring the Raven to handle tough situations they find themselves stuck in. Proficient in tracking, thieving, and combat, their skills are always available to anyone who can pay the price; there is a designated offering box in the Temple of Valdyr where those wishing to meet the Raven can leave a written note proposing a business meeting.

THE RAVEN

Medium humanoid, lawful neutral

Armor Class 15 (studded leather)
Hit Points 78 (12d8 + 24)
Speed 30 ft.

STR	DEX	CON	INT	WIS	CHA
12 (+1)	17 (+3)	14 (+2)	14 (+2)	15 (+2)	13 (+1)

Saving Throws Dex +6, Int +5
Skills Arcana +5, Acrobatics +9, Perception +5, Sleight of Hand +6, Stealth +9
Condition Immunities charmed, disease, frightened, poison
Senses passive Perception 15
Languages Common, Dwarvish, Elvish
Challenge 6 (2,300 XP)

Assassinate. The Raven has advantage on attack rolls against any creature that hasn't taken a turn in the combat yet. In addition, any hit the Raven scores against a creature that is surprised is a critical hit.

Evasion. If the Raven is subjected to an effect that allows them to make a Dexterity saving throw to take only half damage, the Raven instead takes no damage if they succeed on the saving throw, and only half damage if they fail.

Sneak Attack (1/turn). The Raven deals an extra 10 (3d6) damage when they hit a target with a weapon attack and has advantage on the attack roll, or when the target is within 5 feet of an ally of theirs that isn't incapacitated, and the Raven doesn't have disadvantage on the attack roll.

Actions

Multiattack. The Raven makes two melee attacks.
Scimitar. *Melee Weapon Attack:* +6 to hit, reach 5 ft., one target. *Hit:* 6 (1d6 + 3) slashing damage.
Rapier. *Melee Weapon Attack:* +6 to hit, reach 5 ft., one target. *Hit:* 7 (1d8 + 3) piercing damage.
Dagger. *Melee or Ranged Weapon Attack:* +6 to hit, reach 5 ft. or range 20/60 ft., one target. *Hit:* 5 (1d4 + 3) piercing damage
Longbow. *Ranged Weapon Attack:* +6 to hit, range 150/600 ft., one target. *Hit:* 7 (1d8 + 3) piercing damage

Reactions

Uncanny Dodge. The Raven can halve the damage of an attack against them. To do so, they must see the attacker.

As the years have progressed, the Raven has not only become a master thief, but also a merciless killer. Because of the increase in their skillset, their loss of morality, and also because of the fact that they no longer remove their plague doctor mask under any circumstances, some say the current Raven is no longer the original elven rogue, and that the one that is rumored to be striking from the shadows throughout Cat's Cradle is really someone (or something) else that has simply taken up the mantle. Whether or not that is the case, the Raven still acts as a mercenary-for-hire and is willing to do any deed that requires theft, intimidation, maiming, or killing. No longer perturbed by the fact they often get blamed for any random wonton deaths in the city and surrounding locales, the Raven seems to embraced their new moniker of "Angel of Death", using this reputation to their benefit (either by getting more work, or by intimidating payment out of scared individuals).

THE RAVEN

Medium humanoid, neutral evil

Armor Class 20 (natural, *bracers of defense*)
Hit Points 104 (16d8 + 32)
Speed 40 ft.

STR	DEX	CON	INT	WIS	CHA
12 (+1)	20 (+5)	14 (+2)	16 (+3)	17 (+3)	10 (+0)

Saving Throws Dex +9, Int +7
Skills Arcana +7, Acrobatics +13, Perception +7, Sleight of Hand +9, Stealth +13
Condition Immunities charmed, disease, frightened, poison
Senses blindsight 60 ft., passive Perception 17
Languages Abyssal, Celestial, Common, Draconic, Dwarvish, Elvish
Challenge 10 (5,900 XP)

Assassinate. The Raven has advantage on attack rolls against any creature that hasn't taken a turn in the combat yet. In

NO LONGER THE BIRD OF YORE

The original Raven has gone, but their mantle has been upheld by someone else, a very adept Yshkat rogue who uses the reputation previously built up by the original Raven to get work. If the players had any interactions with the original Raven, this new one does not remember nor honor any previous dealings. Whether or not the original Raven is somewhere still alive is up to your discretion.

addition, any hit the Raven scores against a creature that is surprised is a critical hit.

Evasion. If the Raven is subjected to an effect that allows them to make a Dexterity saving throw to take only half damage, the Raven instead takes no damage if they succeed on the saving throw, and only half damage if they fail.

Pounce. If the Raven moves at least 20 feet straight toward a creature and then hits with a melee attack on the same turn, that target must succeed on a DC 13 Strength saving throw or be knocked prone. If the target is prone, the Raven can make one additional melee attack against it as a bonus action.

Reflexive Displacement. The Raven has reflexes that shift their location away from sudden threats, causing attack rolls against it to have disadvantage. If they are hit by an attack, this trait is disrupted until the end of their next turn. This trait is also disrupted while the Raven is incapacitated or has a speed of 0.

Sneak Attack (1/turn). The Raven deals an extra 14 (4d6) damage when they hit a target with a weapon attack and has advantage on the attack roll, or when the target is within 5 feet of an ally of theirs that isn't incapacitated, and the Raven doesn't have disadvantage on the attack roll.

Innate Spellcasting. The Raven's innate spellcasting ability is Intelligence (spell save DC 15, +7 to hit with magical attacks). They can cast the following spells without material components.
At will: *mage hand, mending, shocking grasp*
2/day each: *burning hands, dimension door*
1/day each: *hold person, web*

Special Equipment. The Raven wears *bracers of defense*.

Actions

Multiattack. The Raven makes two melee attacks.

Scimitar. *Melee Weapon Attack:* +9 to hit, reach 5 ft., one target. *Hit:* 8 (1d6 + 5) slashing damage.

Rapier. *Melee Weapon Attack:* +9 to hit, reach 5 ft., one target. *Hit:* 9 (1d8 + 5) piercing damage.

Dagger. *Melee or Ranged Weapon Attack:* +9 to hit, reach 5 ft. or range 20/60 ft., one target. *Hit:* 7 (1d4 + 5) piercing damage

Longbow. *Ranged Weapon Attack:* +9 to hit, range 150/600 ft., one target. *Hit:* 9 (1d8 + 5) piercing damage

Reactions

Uncanny Dodge. The Raven can halve the damage of an attack against them. To do so, they must see the attacker.

Ry'kyna of the Grey Wolves

This muscular human woman is clearly a barbarian because of her hide armor, fur coverings, and dark red woad painted upon her. Over her form-fitted leather cuirass she wears a sleeveless short half-tabard and a large grey wolf pelt cloak over her shoulders. Atop her head covering her braided fair hair is the metal open-faced helm of a knight she slew in single combat.

Ry'kyna of the Grey Wolves is the third daughter (and ninth overall child) of the human Chieftess shieldmaiden Tulris One-Eye and her half-orc husband Greystripe of the mighty Grey Wolf tribe from the Razorback Plains on the far side of the Cantricle Forest. The Grey Wolves are a nomadic clan, and while they are more of a barbaric nature, they actually deal in trade with the pelts and fur they acquire, as well as bone scrimshaw and pieces of arms and armor they take from their fallen enemies. Ry'kyna has loyalty to her family and to her tribe and is content living the life of a warrior. Like the rest of her family, Ry'kyna is notorious for her blind rage on the battlefield, swinging her single-bladed two-handed axe with skill and fury. She is never seen without a weapon nearby, nor without the two horns she carries strapped to her belt: one for signaling battle, and one for drinking alcohol. Menial labor and farming bore her immensely, and she would rather be feasting, fighting, or raiding. That being said, when she gets sent to protect caravans that head to trade hubs (such as Cat's Cradle), Ry'kyna is known to get cantankerous and moody, with the end of any day she wasn't able to get into a fight being filled with a copious amount of drinking.

RY'KYNA OF THE GREY WOLVES
Medium humanoid, chaotic neutral

Armor Class 15 (unarmored defense)
Hit Points 60 (8d8 + 24)
Speed 40 ft.

STR	DEX	CON	INT	WIS	CHA
16 (+3)	14 (+2)	17 (+3)	10 (+1)	13 (+1)	11 (+0)

Saving Throws Str +5, Con +5
Skills Athletics +5, Intimidation +2, Perception +3
Senses passive Perception 13
Languages Common, Orc
Challenge 3 (700 XP)

Brave. Ry'kyna has advantage on saving throws against being frightened.

Danger Sense. Ry'kyna has advantage on Dexterity saving throws against effects that she can see, such as traps and spells. She loses this benefit if she is blinded, deafened, or incapacitated.

Rage (recharges after a short or long rest). As a bonus action, Ry'kyna can enter a rage that lasts for 1 minute. The rage ends early if Ry'kyna is knocked unconscious or if her turn ends and she hasn't attacked a hostile creature or taken damage since her last turn. While raging, Ry'kyna gains the following benefits:
• She has advantage on Strength checks and Strength saving throws.
• She deals an extra 2 damage when she hits a target with a melee weapon attack.
• She has resistance to bludgeoning, piercing, and slashing damage.
• She may use a bonus action to make a single melee attack.
• She cannot be charmed or frightened. If she was charmed or

frightened when entering her rage, the effect is suspended for the duration of the rage.

Actions

Multiattack. Ry'kyna makes two melee attacks.
Greataxe. *Melee Weapon Attack:* +5 to hit, reach 5 ft., one target.
 Hit: 9 (1d12 + 3) slashing damage.
Javelin. *Ranged Weapon Attack:* +5 to hit, range 30/120 ft., one target. *Hit:* 6 (1d6 + 3) piercing damage

Ry'kyna the barbarian has gotten over her weariness of being a simple "guard dog" for the basic merchant caravans that travel along the trade routes of the region. Instead, she has come to realize that it is riskier roads or the wagons carrying the most valuable goods that incur the greatest possible chance of an ambush taking place... and that is the type of chaos and violence she wishes to test her mettle against. Having left the relative calm of protecting her own people, who were more than capable of defending themselves without her, Ry'kyna opts now for the most dangerous assignments. She is even part of a betting pool at the Brackish Moon tavern in the Old Town district of Cat's Cradle: whichever mercenary brings the most fangs, ears, or fingerbones of things they've killed within a week gets free drinks all night.

RY'KYNA OF THE GREY WOLVES

Medium humanoid, chaotic neutral

Armor Class 15 (unarmored defense)
Hit Points 90 (12d8 + 36)
Speed 40 ft.

STR	DEX	CON	INT	WIS	CHA
16 (+3)	15 (+2)	17 (+3)	10 (+1)	13 (+1)	11 (+0)

Saving Throws Str +6, Con +6
Skills Athletics +6, Intimidation +3, Perception +4
Senses passive Perception 14
Languages Common, Orc
Challenge 6 (2,300 XP)

Brave. Ry'kyna has advantage on saving throws against being frightened.
Danger Sense. Ry'kyna has advantage on Dexterity saving throws against effects that she can see, such as traps and spells. She loses this benefit if she is blinded, deafened, or incapacitated.
Feral Instinct. Ry'kyna has advantage on initiative rolls. In addition, if she is surprised at the beginning of combat and isn't incapacitated, she can act normally on her first turn, but only if she enters her rage before doing anything else on that turn.
Rage (recharges after a short or long rest). As a bonus action, Ry'kyna can enter a rage that lasts for 1 minute. The rage ends early if Ry'kyna is knocked unconscious or if her turn ends and she hasn't attacked a hostile creature or taken damage since her last turn. While raging, Ry'kyna gains the following benefits:
• She has advantage on Strength checks and Strength saving throws.
• She deals an extra 3 damage when she hits a target with a melee weapon attack.
• She has resistance to bludgeoning, piercing, and slashing damage.
• She may can use a bonus action to make a single melee attack.
• She cannot be charmed or frightened. If she was charmed or frightened when entering her rage, the effect is suspended for the duration of the rage.
• If she drops to 0 hit points while she is raging and didn't die outright, she can make a DC 10 Constitution saving throw. If she succeeds, she drops to 1 hit point instead. Each time she uses this feature after the first, the DC increases by 5. When she finishes a short or long rest, the DC resets to 10.

Actions

Multiattack. Ry'kyna makes two melee attacks.
Greataxe. *Melee Weapon Attack:* +6 to hit, reach 5 ft., one target.

Hit: 9 (1d12 +3) slashing damage.
Javelin. *Ranged Weapon Attack:* +6 to hit, range 30/120 ft., one target. *Hit:* 6 (1d6+3) piercing damage

Ry'kyna of the Grey Wolves sits on the patio of a local tavern, wearing her worn mithril cuirass with her weapons laid out on the table before her, and angrily counts the coin she has remaining in her pouch. Anyone who keeps up with local rumor knows the tale: the barbarian woman has traveled far from her homeland back to Cat's Cradle in order to find the alchemist who sold her tribe cursed potions and salts that has caused a plague to decimate her people. No one has been able to help her, either because they are too afraid or because there have been no leads to help in the investigation. Ry'kyna has very little information to go by for her quest: a strip of black cloth with red threading, a fragment of a scroll with mysterious abstract runes written in blue ink, and a map of a cave system with no discernable markings. She is looking for anyone with information about curses, incurable illness, backfiring potions, or anything that can lead her to what she seeks.

RY'KYNA OF THE GREY WOLVES

Medium humanoid, chaotic neutral

Armor Class 15 (unarmored defense)
Hit Points 120 (16d8 + 48)
Speed 40 ft.

STR	DEX	CON	INT	WIS	CHA
16 (+3)	15 (+2)	17 (+3)	10 (+1)	13 (+1)	11 (+0)

Saving Throws Str +7, Con +7
Skills Athletics +7, Intimidation +4, Perception +5
Senses passive Perception 15
Languages Common, Orc
Challenge 10 (5,900 XP)

Brave. Ry'kyna has advantage on saving throws against being frightened.
Danger Sense. Ry'kyna has advantage on Dexterity saving throws against effects that she can see, such as traps and spells. She loses this benefit if she is blinded, deafened, or incapacitated.
Feral Instinct. Ry'kyna has advantage on initiative rolls. In addition, if she is surprised at the beginning of combat and isn't incapacitated, she can act normally on her first turn, but only if she enters her rage before doing anything else on that turn.
Rage (recharges after a short or long rest). As a bonus action, Ry'kyna can enter a rage that lasts for 1 minute. The rage ends early if Ry'kyna is knocked unconscious or if she chooses to end it. While raging, Ry'kyna gains the following benefits:
• She has advantage on Strength checks and Strength saving throws.
• She deals an extra 4 damage when she hits a target with a melee weapon attack.
• She has resistance to bludgeoning, piercing, and slashing damage.
• She may use a bonus action to make a single melee attack.
• She cannot be charmed or frightened. If she was charmed or frightened when entering her rage, the effect is suspended for the duration of the rage.
• If she drops to 0 hit points while she is raging and didn't die outright, she can make a DC 10 Constitution saving throw. If she succeeds, she drops to 1 hit point instead. Each time she uses this feature after the first, the DC increases by 5. When she finishes a short or long rest, the DC resets to 10.

Actions

Multiattack. Ry'kyna makes two melee attacks.
Greataxe. *Melee Weapon Attack:* +7 to hit, reach 5 ft., one target.
 Hit: 9 (1d12 +3) slashing damage.
Javelin. *Ranged Weapon Attack:* +7 to hit, range 30/120 ft., one target. *Hit:* 6 (1d6+3) piercing damage.
Intimidating Presence. Rykyna chooses one creature that she can see within 30 ft. of her. If the creature can see or hear her, it must succeed on a Wisdom saving throw DC 12 or be frightened

of her until the end of her next turn. On subsequent turns, she can use her action to extend the duration of this effect on the frightened creature until the end of her next turn. This effect ends if the creature ends its turn out of line of sight or more than 60 ft. away from Ry'kyna. If the creature succeeds on its saving throw, Ry'kyna can't use this feature on that creature again for 24 hours.

SARGASH UTHAK

Sargash Uthak is an up-and-coming mariner on Hyon Lake, captain of the trim schooner Doleful Wanderer and part-owner in several others. Flamboyant, outgoing, and loud, Sargash attracts others of his kind, who all have good hearts but little respect for the law. He revels in adventure, for though Hyon is well isolated from the high seas, it is nevertheless a dangerous place, plagued by fearsome lake monsters and even its own breed of corsairs who prey upon the lucrative trade routes between Cat's Cradle and lakeside towns and villages.

Sargash himself has been sailing for nearly a decade, starting off as an assistant deckhand and cabin boy and rising through the ranks to become first mate of a large merchant ship. His background is somewhat spotty, including stints of smuggling and even an occasional flirtation with outright piracy when he lived on the seacoast years ago. Today he maintains a relatively lawful existence, but he is not above occasionally returning to his old ways, smuggling contraband in and out of Cat's Cradle, bribing the odd official or sabotaging competitors whom he feels haven't played him fair.

Sargash's history is a bit spotty

CAPTAIN SARGASH UTHAK

Medium humanoid (orc), chaotic good

Armor Class 13 (studded leather)
Hit Points 90 (12d8 + 36)
Speed 30 ft.

STR	DEX	CON	INT	WIS	CHA
18 (+4)	12 (+1)	16 (+3)	13 (+1)	11 (+0)	14 (+2)

Saving Throws Str +6, Con +5
Skills Athletics +8, Intimidation +6, Medicine +4, Perception +4, Persuasion +6, Stealth +5, Survival +4
Senses darkvision 60 ft. passive Perception 14
Languages Common, Orcish
Challenge 3 (700 XP)

Actions

Greataxe. *Melee Weapon Attack:* +6 to hit, reach 5 ft., one target. *Hit:* 10 (1d12 + 4) slashing damage.
Spear. *Melee or Ranged Weapon Attack:* +6 to hit, reach 5 ft. or range 20/60 ft., one target. *Hit:* 7 (1d6 + 4) piercing damage, or 11 (2d6 + 4) piercing damage if used with two hands to make a melee attack.

Years on the lake have transformed Sargash into a veteran Hyon captain, with a small fleet of ships and crews of experienced sailors. He doesn't go out on trade runs as much as he used to but instead spends more time managing his business from his floating headquarters aboard the refitted *Doleful Wayfarer.* He maintains a love-hate relationship with the law, and still engages in questionable activities, but his basically good nature remains. Nevertheless, he has encountered a great deal of prejudice against non-humans and has been known to use these prejudices to his advantage, feigning murderous rages and threatening those who stand in his way. For the most part, his displays are all bark and no bite and usually succeed in getting Sargash his way.

Sargash has also become a more flamboyant character, dressing in feathered hats and sporting piratical weapons at his side, though he rarely uses them. He broke his tusks in an accident several years ago when he was struck in the face by an out of control boom. One of his tusks has been capped with gold, while the other he leaves broken and jagged as a reminder to him and his crews to always be wary. In the course of his various exploits, Sargash has obtained a set of *+2 mariner's studded leather,* and an old dwarven *+1 greataxe.*

CAPTAIN SARGASH UTHAK

Medium humanoid (orc), chaotic good

Armor Class 15 (*+2 mariner's studded leather*)
Hit Points 120 (16d8 + 48)
Speed 30 ft., swim 30 ft.

STR	DEX	CON	INT	WIS	CHA
18 (+4)	12 (+1)	16 (+3)	13 (+1)	11 (+0)	14 (+2)

Saving Throws Str +7, Con +6
Skills Athletics +10, Intimidation +8, Medicine +6, Perception +6, Persuasion +8, Stealth +7, Survival +6
Senses darkvision 60 ft. passive Perception 16
Languages Common, Dwarvish, Orcish
Challenge 6 (2300 XP)

Actions

+1 Greataxe. *Melee Weapon Attack:* +8 to hit, reach 5 ft., one target. *Hit:* 11 (1d12 + 5) slashing damage.
Spear. *Melee or Ranged Weapon Attack:* +7 to hit, reach 5 ft. or range 20/60 ft., one target. *Hit:* 7 (1d6 + 4) piercing damage, or 11 (2d6 + 4) piercing damage if used with two hands to make a melee attack.

An aging grizzled but still vital and often dangerous individual, Sargash continues to manage a large fleet of lake vessels and has grown quite prosperous. He is an even more powerful combatant and has added a *ring of protection* to his collection of magical items. He has never married or had children and continues to manage his business aboard the *Doleful Wayfarer.* Some of his current isolation and his drift away from his old good-heartedness may be attributed to the fact that he now carries a secret curse.

During one of his increasingly-rare expeditions across the lake to transport volatile and expensive alchemical reactants, Sargash was ambushed by a small fleet of corsairs in light, fast vessels who attempted to swarm the *Doleful Wayfarer* and plunder its valuable cargo. Sargash met the corsair's leader, a half-ogre with a fearsome blood-covered axe in battle and prevailed despite near-mortal wounds. Upon recovery Sargash took the axe as his own, never realizing that it was actually a *berserker's axe* and that now he values it above all other possessions. Unaware of the axe's fearsome powers, Sargash led another voyage across the lake the following spring, with his first mate Synaela, a half-elven mariner, someone for whom Sargash had, for the first time, felt true love. As luck would have it, the *Wayfarer* was again attacked by corsairs, but as Sargash and Synaela fought side-by-side on the deck, he was wounded by a pirate and went berserk, cutting down Synaela before the attackers were finally defeated.

Grief-stricken, Sargash retained enough sense to realize the full horror of what had happened, and subsequent research proved to him that the axe was indeed cursed, yet he still cannot rid himself of it. He has determined never to go out on the lake again and to avoid combat at all costs, lest he inflict further tragedy on himself and others. His old goodness has been replaced by gruff wariness and increasing paranoia, though he still holds out a faint hope that someone will be able to rid him of his terrible curse.

CAPTAIN SARGASH UTHAK

Medium humanoid (orc), chaotic neutral

Armor Class 16 (+2 *mariner's studded leather, ring of protection*)
Hit Points 209 (22d8 + 88 + 22 from the *berserker axe*)
Speed 30 ft.

STR	DEX	CON	INT	WIS	CHA
18 (+4)	12 (+1)	18 (+4)	14 (+2)	11 (+0)	14 (+2)

Saving Throws Str +8, Con +8
Skills Athletics +12, History +10, Intimidation +10, Medicine +8, Perception +8, Persuasion +10, Stealth +9, Survival +8
Senses darkvision 60 ft. passive Perception 18
Languages Common, Dwarvish, Orcish
Challenge 10 (5900 XP)

Ring of Protection. Sargash has a +1 bonus to all saving throws.

Actions

Berserker Axe. *Melee Weapon Attack:* +9 to hit, reach 5 ft., one target. *Hit:* 11 (1d12 + 5) slashing damage.

Spear. *Melee or Ranged Weapon Attack:* +8 to hit, reach 5 ft. or range 20/60 ft., one target. *Hit:* 7 (1d6 + 4) piercing damage, or 11 (2d6 + 4) piercing damage if used with two hands to make a melee attack.

VAL KADEN

An attractive human in their late-30s leans up against the side of a covered wagon. With a pale freckled face and pinned back brilliant curly red hair, they are wearing a smart leather jerkin, with matching leather skirt and boots, but it is their long multi-colored cape that draws your attention; its swirling patterns make you think of the starry night sky, of a field of poppies and dandelions, of a rushing river, a thunderstorm, an explosion of fire… you blink your eyes and look up into their smiling face. "A silver for the show, love. And that includes one free drink!"

In their youth, Val Kaden was born into a nomadic tribe of con artists and deceivers that performed false miracles, set up rigged games of chance, and offered contrived fortune tellings, all in the effort to fool the common folk of the land and steal the meager amount money they had scraped together. With their naturally bright red hair and attractive features, the tribe had hoped to train them up to be a skilled con artist, wooing marks out of their wealth. But Val had other plans: they wanted to travel the lands, let out into the world the music they heard in their soul, and instead of stealing from the folk they met, offer legitimate hope and uplifting moods. Ah, the naiveté of youth… Years later, a down-on-their-luck Val found themselves in the city of Cat's Cradle, performing at any inn or tavern they could in order scrape together enough to pay for a room and food. Always seeking work, and keeping an eye for any odd jobs, they will always have a few rumors at the ready for things going on in or around town.

VAL KADEN

Medium humanoid, chaotic good

Armor Class 14 (leather)
Hit Points 44 (8d8 + 8)

Speed 30 ft.

STR	DEX	CON	INT	WIS	CHA
11 (+0)	16 (+3)	12 (+1)	15 (+2)	13 (+1)	17 (+3)

Saving Throws Dex +5, Cha +5
Skills Acrobatics +7, Insight +5, Performance +7, Persuade +7, Sleight of Hand +5
Senses passive Perception 11
Languages Common, Dwarvish, Elvish
Challenge 3 (700 XP)

Cunning Action. On each of their turns, Val can use a bonus action to take the Dash, Disengage, Hide, or Use an Object action. In addition, this bonus action can be used to make a Dexterity (Sleight of Hand) check to use their thieves' tools to disarm a trap or open a lock.

Sneak Attack (1/turn). Val deals an extra 7 (2d6) damage when they hit a target with a weapon attack and has advantage on the attack roll, or when the target is within 5 feet of an ally of theirs that isn't incapacitated, and Val doesn't have disadvantage on the attack roll.

Spellcasting. Val is a 5th-level spellcaster. Their spellcasting ability is Charisma (spell save DC 13, +5 to hit with spell attacks). They have the following bard spells prepared:
Cantrips (at will): *light, mage hand, vicious mockery*
1st level (4 slots): *detect magic, healing word, heroism, hideous laughter*
2nd level (3 slots): *calm emotions, detect thoughts, silence*
3rd level (2 slots): *hypnotic pattern*

Actions

Scimitar. *Melee Weapon Attack:* +5 to hit, reach 5 ft., one target. *Hit:* 6 (1d6 + 3) slashing damage.

Dagger. *Melee or Ranged Weapon Attack:* +5 to hit, reach 5 ft. or range 20/60 ft., one target. *Hit:* 5 (1d4 + 3) piercing damage.

Shortbow. Ranged Weapon Attack: +5 to hit, range 80/320 ft., one target. *Hit:* 6 (1d6 + 3) piercing damage.

Val Kaden is an established bard of moderate renown in the city of Cat's Cradle, performing occasionally at the more well-known establishments, even including a place or two in the Jade District, but can primarily be found at the Rebellious Boggart in the Gold District. Val themself has regained a level of optimism about the world and is always on the lookout to do a good deed for the downtrodden. While they would never go up directly against any of the criminal groups in Old Town, Val always seems to be able to direct city guard or do-good adventurers in a direction that would disrupt a criminal enterprise or the like. Occasionally Val leads a small group that they refer to as their "band" to do a bit of "adventuring" themselves outside of the city, typically if it comes to acquiring a lost or stolen object or fending off a troublesome creature harassing local farmers or mining groups. Most of the city guards appreciate this work that Val does, and pass along leads or rumors that they cannot follow up on themselves.

VAL KADEN

Medium humanoid, chaotic good

Armor Class 16 (chain shirt)
Hit Points 66 (12d8 + 12)
Speed 30 ft.

STR	DEX	CON	INT	WIS	CHA
11 (+0)	16 (+3)	12 (+1)	15 (+2)	14 (+2)	18 (+4)

Saving Throws Dex +6, Cha +7
Skills Acrobatics +9, Arcana +5, Insight +8, Performance +10, Persuade +10, Sleight of Hand +6
Senses passive Perception 12
Languages Common, Dwarvish, Elvish
Challenge 6 (2,300 XP)

Cunning Action. On each of their turns, Val can use a bonus action to take the Dash, Disengage, Hide, or Use an Object action. In addition, this bonus action can be used to make a Dexterity (Sleight of Hand) check to use their thieves' tools to disarm a trap or open a lock.

Sneak Attack (1/turn). Val deals an extra 10 (3d6) damage when they hit a target with a weapon attack and has advantage on the attack roll, or when the target is within 5 feet of an ally of theirs that isn't incapacitated, and Val doesn't have disadvantage on the attack roll.

Spellcasting. Val is a 7th-level spellcaster. Their spellcasting ability is Charisma (spell save DC 15, +7 to hit with spell attacks). They have the following bard spells prepared:
Cantrips (at will): *light, mage hand, vicious mockery*
1st level (4 slots): *detect magic, healing word, heroism, hideous laughter*
2nd level (3 slots): *calm emotions, detect thoughts, silence*
3rd level (3 slots): *hypnotic pattern, major image*
4th level (1 slots): *confusion*

Actions

Multiattack. Val makes two melee attacks or two ranged attacks.
Scimitar. *Melee Weapon Attack:* +6 to hit, reach 5 ft., one target. *Hit:* 6 (1d6 + 3) slashing damage.
Dagger. *Melee or Ranged Weapon Attack:* +6 to hit, reach 5 ft. or range 20/60 ft., one target. *Hit:* 5 (1d4 + 3) piercing damage.
Shortbow. *Ranged Weapon Attack:* +6 to hit, range 80/320 ft., one target. *Hit:* 6 (1d6 + 3) piercing damage.

Reactions

Uncanny Dodge. Val can halve the damage of an attack against them. To do so, they must see the attacker.

Val Kaden is now the leader of a roaming entertainment group calling themselves the "Exemplarily Scramacious Twilight Troupe". While they still consider Cat's Cradle to be their "home" (for lack of a better term), the band travels tirelessly on all the surrounding roads and caravan routes: to Voles and Dancers to the north and south, and to Five-and-Copper and Sundry to the east and west, respectfully. They entertain with their magic shows, acrobatic performances, feats of physical amazement, and humorous tales of adventure. Val makes sure that any "games of chance" offered by the troupe are not rigged in their favor, and instead are a legitimate test of skill or wit. The troupe has acquired enough of a reputation that they are not mistaken for a band of thieves, but they still prefer to set up camp outside of most city walls, only entering town to obtain food and supplies. Val has made sure to employ numerous scouts and hunters that protect the group when they travel and also serve as guards when they establish camp near a location where coin can be obtained from the populace. When the troupe finds itself set up outside the walls of Cat's Cradle (which it often is), Val will occasionally pop into town to visit the Rebellious Boggart, where they used to work, and keeps a pleasant relationship with the owner. While Val does more managing and organizing these days, they do still occasionally perform as a special occurrence for particularly wealthy or invigorated audiences. Val is always willing to have an audience with almost anyone to hear whatever proposition they wish to present to them (or their troupe) but rarely do they seek anyone out themselves for any jobs.

VAL KADEN

Medium humanoid, chaotic good

Armor Class 17 (breastplate)
Hit Points 88 (16d8 + 16)
Speed 30 ft.

STR	DEX	CON	INT	WIS	CHA
11 (+0)	16 (+3)	12 (+1)	15 (+2)	14 (+2)	20 (+5)

Saving Throws Dex +7, Cha +9
Skills Acrobatics +11, Arcana +6, History +6, Insight +10, Performance +13, Persuade +13, Religion +6, Sleight of Hand +7
Senses passive Perception 12
Languages Common, Dwarvish, Elvish
Challenge 10 (5,900 XP)

Cunning Action. On each of their turns, Val can use a bonus action to take the Dash, Disengage, Hide, or Use an Object action. In addition, this bonus action can be used to make a Dexterity (Sleight of Hand) check to use their thieves' tools to disarm a trap or open a lock.

Evasion. If Val is subjected to an effect that allows them to make a Dexterity saving throw to take only half damage, Val instead takes no damage if they succeed on the saving throw, and only half damage if they fail.

Sneak Attack (1/turn). Val deals an extra 14 (4d6) damage when they hit a target with a weapon attack and has advantage on the attack roll, or when the target is within 5 feet of an ally of theirs that isn't incapacitated, and Val doesn't have disadvantage on the attack roll.

Spellcasting. Val is a 9th-level spellcaster. Their spellcasting ability is Charisma (spell save DC 17, +9 to hit with spell attacks). They have the following bard spells prepared:
Cantrips (at will): *light, mage hand, vicious mockery*
1st level (4 slots): *detect magic, healing word, heroism, hideous laughter*
2nd level (3 slots): *calm emotions, detect thoughts, silence*
3rd level (3 slots): *hypnotic pattern, major image*
4th level (3 slots): *confusion, greater invisibility*
5th level (1 slot): *scrying*

Actions

Multiattack. Val makes two melee attacks or two ranged attacks.
Scimitar. *Melee Weapon Attack:* +7 to hit, reach 5 ft., one target. *Hit:* 6 (1d6 + 3) slashing damage.
Dagger. *Melee or Ranged Weapon Attack:* +7 to hit, reach 5 ft. or range 20/60 ft., one target. *Hit:* 5 (1d4 + 3) piercing damage.
Shortbow. *Ranged Weapon Attack:* +7 to hit, range 80/320 ft., one target. *Hit:* 6 (1d6 + 3) piercing damage.

Reactions

Uncanny Dodge. Val can halve the damage of an attack against them. To do so, they must see the attacker.

VALDRIN HOFF

Valdrin is a serious and hard-bitten individual who rarely smiles, but who retains a deep sense of right and wrong. Orphaned in infancy, he grew up in a series of orphanages and workhouses, learning to survive by his wits and with his fists, while also gaining a deep understanding and affection for the lowly and the downtrodden in society. As a young man, he joined the city watch in a large city, only to be appalled by the corruption and uncaring attitude of his colleagues. After learning as many skills as he could — including learning multiple languages, gaining expertise with hand crossbows and the secrets of disabling hostile spellcasters — Valdrin quit the watch and made his way to Cat's Cradle, where he set himself up in the Ovens, providing security and aiding locals who were ignored by the City Watch, particularly in the Ovens and the Old City.

Today Hoff continues his trade, operating out of a small, run-down apartment. He has been instrumental in solving a number of important crimes throughout Cat's Cradle, but this is not widely known as he often prefers to hand out justice personally, rather than rely upon the City Watch, whom he considers little better than the corrupt organization in his former home. On the other hand, Hoff and the members of the Constabulary have developed a grudging mutual respect over the years. Hoff's contacts within the Constabulary often share information with him and usually turn a blind eye to his extra-legal activities. For his part, Hoff allows some criminals to be taken into custody if supervised by the Constabulary.

VALDRIN HOFF

Medium humanoid (human), neutral good

Armor Class 15 (leather coat)
Hit Points 67 (15d8)
Speed 30 ft.

STR	DEX	CON	INT	WIS	CHA
13 (+1)	14 (+2)	10 (+0)	15 (+2)	16 (+3)	14 (+2)

Saving Throws Dex +4, Wis +5

Skills Acrobatics +4, Deception +4, History +4, Insight +5, Intimidation +4, Investigation +4, Medicine +5, Perception +5, Persuasion +4, Sleight of Hand +4, Stealth +4
Senses passive Perception 15
Languages Common, Dwarvish, Elvish, Goblin, Halfling, Orc
Challenge 3 (700 XP)

Hard-boiled. Valdrin has advantage on Charisma (Intimidation) checks and on saving throws against confusion and against being frightened or charmed.
Mage Slayer. When a creature within 5 feet of Valdrin casts a spell, he can use his reaction to make a melee weapon attack against that creature. If he damages a creature that is concentrating on a spell, that creature has disadvantage on the saving throw it makes to maintain its concentration.
Man of a Thousand Faces. Valdrin gained extensive skill in disguise during his years on the city watch, and today can change his own appearance and that of his clothing, weapons, and armor. He can appear up to six inches taller or shorter, and can appear thin, fat, or in between. His disguises automatically succeed against casual observers, and anyone who inspects him closely must succeed on a DC 13 Intelligence (Investigation) check to see through the deception.
My Crossbow is Quick. Valdrin can wield two hand crossbows simultaneously and can make one attack with each per round. The first attack is made normally, the second at a −2 penalty to Valdrin's attack roll.

Actions

Hand Crossbow. *Ranged Weapon Attack:* +4 to hit, range 30/120 ft., one target. *Hit:* 5 (1d6 + 2) piercing damage
Longsword. *Melee Weapon Attack:* +3 to hit, reach 5 ft., one target. *Hit:* 5 (1d8 + 1) slashing damage or 6 (1d10 + 1) slashing damage if used with two hands

The years have sharpened Hoff's reflexes and skills, as well as making him an especially feared nemesis of criminals across Cat's Cradle, especially the operatives of the Kennick Syndicate. After several run-ins, Hoff is determined to bring the syndicate down whatever it takes and has even begun to pursue some of his own independent investigations of the organization's smuggling and protection schemes. He has forged a close professional relationship with Inspector Mattea Theasen, who has been helping him surreptitiously and keeping her actions secret from her superiors.

Valdrin also shuns the use of magic and magical items in his investigations, though he has a number of spellcasting allies whom he turns to when needed. A recent job for a number of fae whose clan relic had been stolen has also led to good relations with the fair folk, whom he also occasionally calls upon to aid him in his investigations. Prominent among his fae allies are Starshine, a mischievous but loyal and determined **blink dog**, and a band of **sprites** led by the warrior Daeg.

VALDRIN HOFF

Medium humanoid (human), neutral good

Armor Class 16 (leather coat)
Hit Points 99 (22d8)
Speed 30 ft.

STR	DEX	CON	INT	WIS	CHA
13 (+1)	16 (+3)	10 (+0)	15 (+2)	16 (+3)	14 (+2)

Saving Throws Dex +6, Wis +6
Skills Acrobatics +6, Deception +5, History +5, Insight +6, Intimidation +5, Investigation +5, Medicine +6, Perception +6, Persuasion +5, Sleight of Hand +6, Stealth +6
Senses passive Perception 16
Languages Common, Dwarvish, Elvish, Goblin, Halfling, Orc, Sylvan
Challenge 6 (2300 XP)

Hard-boiled. Valdrin has advantage on Charisma (Intimidation) checks and on saving throws against confusion and against being frightened or charmed.

Mage Slayer. When a creature within 5 feet of Valdrin casts
a spell, he can use his reaction to make a melee weapon
attack against that creature. If he damages a creature that is
concentrating on a spell, that creature has disadvantage on the
saving throw it makes to maintain its concentration.

Man of a Thousand Faces. Valdrin gained extensive skill in
disguise during his years on the city watch, and today can
change his own appearance and that of his clothing, weapons
and armor. He can appear up to six inches taller or shorter, and
can appear thin, fat or in between. His disguises automatically
succeed against casual observers, and anyone who inspects him
closely must succeed on a DC 16 Intelligence (Investigation)
check to see through the deception.

My Crossbow is Quick. Valdrin can wield two hand crossbows
simultaneously and can make one attack with each per round.
The first attack is made normally, the second at a −2 penalty to
Valdrin's attack roll.

Actions

Hand Crossbow. Ranged Weapon Attack: +6 to hit, range 30/120
ft., one target. *Hit:* 6 (1d6 + 3) piercing damage

Longsword. Melee Weapon Attack: +4 to hit, reach 5 ft., one
target. *Hit:* 5 (1d8 + 1) slashing damage or 6 (1d10 + 1) slashing
damage if used with two hands

At the height of his abilities and influence, Valdrin remains the defender of
the common folk that he always was. His conflict with the Kennick Syndicate
has grown to a full-scale war, and though a single investigator facing down
with an entrenched criminal organization may seem like a one-sided and
hopeless crusade, Valdrin soldiers on. Despite appearances to the contrary
he is not alone, for he has his allies in the Constabulary and his fae friends
who have grown even more protective and loyal over the years. He has also
developed a network of informers and assistants throughout the city of Cat's
Cradle that includes beggars, shopkeepers, laborers, and even a few petty
criminals, all of whom keep him informed about the activities of the Thieves'
Guild and the Kennick Syndicate, keeping him always a bare step ahead of
those who wish to destroy him.

VALDRIN HOFF

Medium humanoid (human), neutral good

Armor Class 16 (leather coat)
Hit Points 126 (28d8)
Speed 30 ft.

STR	DEX	CON	INT	WIS	CHA
13 (+1)	16 (+3)	10 (+0)	15 (+2)	18 (+4)	14 (+2)

Saving Throws Dex +6, Wis +6
Skills Acrobatics +7, Deception +6, History +6, Insight +8,
Intimidation +6, Investigation +6, Medicine +8, Perception +8,
Persuasion +6, Sleight of Hand +7, Stealth +7
Senses passive Perception 18
Languages Common, Dwarvish, Elvish, Goblin, Halfling, Orc,
Sylvan
Challenge 10 (5900 XP)

Hard-boiled. Valdrin has advantage on Charisma (Intimidation)
checks and on saving throws against confusion and against
being frightened or charmed.

Mage Slayer. When a creature within 5 feet of Valdrin casts
a spell, he can use his reaction to make a melee weapon
attack against that creature. If he damages a creature that is
concentrating on a spell, that creature has disadvantage on the
saving throw it makes to maintain its concentration.

Man of a Thousand Faces. Valdrin gained extensive skill in
disguise during his years on the city watch, and today can
change his own appearance and that of his clothing, weapons
and armor. He can appear up to six inches taller or shorter, and
can appear thin, fat or in between. His disguises automatically
succeed against casual observers, and anyone who inspects him
closely must succeed on a DC 20 Intelligence (Investigation)
check to see through the deception.

Actions

Multiattack. Valdrin makes two longsword or two hand-crossbow
attacks.

Hand Crossbow. Ranged Weapon Attack: +7 to hit, range 30/120
ft., one target. *Hit:* 6 (1d6 + 3) piercing damage

Longsword. Melee Weapon Attack: +5 to hit, reach 5 ft., one
target. *Hit:* 5 (1d8 + 1) slashing damage or 6 (1d10 + 1) slashing
damage if used with two hands

ZOË TORANNO

*This full-bodied half-orc woman is made of pure muscle and intimidation.
Her bronze skin glistens in the sun, as she pulls the ship ropes off of the dock
with a satisfied grunt. Her black mohawk stands prominently on its own, and
the shaved sides of her head are tattooed with intricate purple and red designs.
The necklace around her neck and the sleeveless, armored vest she wears are
adorned with the fangs, claws, and bones of numerous predators she has slain
in combat. Strangely though, on her left wrist she wears a single, unchained,
manacle emblazoned with a faintly glowing triangular rune.*

No one knows Zoe's original homeland, but many speculated based on her
tales that it is far to the south, where dragons are said to still roam free. Forced
in servitude at a very young age, Zoë grew strong through manual labor and
learned quickly about the cruelty of men in the world. After several years of
captivity, she finally saw her opportunity to escape; when her captors failed
to return after they left her in a desolate iron mine, she convinced her guards
to abandon their duties, free her, and make for the nearest town. She doesn't
talk about the journey to freedom, but she does tell people that she alone came
out on the other end. A smart and strong woman needing to disappear and
abandon the area, she signed onto a seafaring crew bound northward, and
off she went. She jumped crews from time to time, making her way farther
northward, before heading inland with a band of insurgents looking to unseat a
local tyrant. Unsuccessful and on her own again, Zoë traversed the wilderness
before coming across the town of Dancers. From there, she eventually found
herself in Cat's Cradle. Working the docks or signing up for a ship's crew, the
strong half-orc woman is up to any challenge. She is always willing to lend a
helping hand to those who need it and has vowed to fight against slavery and

injustice whenever she encounters it.

ZOË TORANNO

Medium humanoid, neutral good

Armor Class 15 (scale mail)
Hit Points 68 (8d8 + 32)
Speed 30 ft.

STR	DEX	CON	INT	WIS	CHA
17 (+3)	13 (+1)	18 (+4)	11 (+0)	12 (+1)	13 (+1)

Saving Throws Str +5, Con +6
Skills Athletics +5, Intimidation +3, Perception +3, Persuasion +3
Senses passive Perception 13
Languages Common, Orc
Challenge 3 (700 XP)

Brave. Zoë has advantage on saving throws against being frightened.

Sneak Attack (1/turn). Zoë deals an extra 7 (2d6) damage when she hits a target with a weapon attack and has advantage on the attack roll, or when the target is within 5 feet of an ally of theirs that isn't incapacitated, and Zoë doesn't have disadvantage on the attack roll.

Actions

Multiattack. Zoë makes two melee attacks or two ranged attacks.

Maul. Melee Weapon Attack: +5 to hit, reach 5 ft., one target. *Hit:* 10 (2d6 + 3) bludgeoning damage.

Handaxe. Melee or Ranged Weapon Attack: +5 to hit, reach 5 ft. or range 30/120 ft., one target. *Hit:* 6 (1d6 + 3) slashing damage.

Zoë is well known throughout the Docks and Old Town of Cat's Cradle for her booming laugh and standoffish attitude. When she and whatever crew she is part of (usually a ship, but sometimes a caravan) arrive in town, they are known to rent out an entire tavern and offer to buy numerous rounds throughout the night. She cares not for treasures or riches, just a good set of gear to fight her enemies, and more importantly, defend those who cannot defend themselves. Zoë has a tense relationship with the guards of the city, as well as certain members of the criminal underworld, as she feels their living conditions and opportunities for honest work could always be better than what they currently are. She is always on the lookout to expose and stop corruption that she sees as a cancer spreading when left unchecked.

ZOË TORANNO

Medium humanoid, neutral good

Armor Class 15 (scale mail)
Hit Points 106 (12d8 +48)
Speed 30 ft.

STR	DEX	CON	INT	WIS	CHA
17 (+3)	14 (+2)	18 (+4)	11 (+0)	12 (+1)	13 (+1)

Saving Throws Str +6, Con +7
Skills Athletics +6, Intimidation +4, Perception +4, Persuasion +4
Senses passive Perception 14
Languages Common, Orc
Challenge 6 (2,300 XP)

Brave. Zoë has advantage on saving throws against being frightened.

Brute. A melee weapon deals one extra die of its damage when Zoë hits with it (included in the attack).

Sneak Attack (1/turn). Zoë deals an extra 10 (3d6) damage when she hits a target with a weapon attack and has advantage on the attack roll, or when the target is within 5 feet of an ally of theirs that isn't incapacitated, and Zoë doesn't have disadvantage on the attack roll.

Actions

Multiattack. Zoë makes two melee attacks or two ranged attacks.

Maul. Melee Weapon Attack: +6 to hit, reach 5 ft., one target. *Hit:* 13 (3d6 + 3) bludgeoning damage.

Handaxe. Melee or Ranged Weapon Attack: +6 to hit, reach 5 ft. or range 30/120 ft., one target. *Hit:* 10 (2d6 + 3) slashing damage.

Drink Up Me Hearties. Zoë can issue a special command or warning to all allied creatures that she can see within 30 feet. For 1 minutes whenever any of those creatures makes an ability check, attack roll, or saving throw, they can add a d4 to their roll provided they can hear and understand Zoë. This effect ends if Zoë is incapacitated.

As a captain aboard the boat *The Unchained Shark,* Zoë is one of the many who handles the imports and exports of the city via the waterways. She had earned a reputation of being honest and fair when it comes to her transporting and rates, and woe betide any who try to take them in a fight. Not only that, but she is known to take the *Shark* and go hunting for river pirates or bandit camps that have been established on the water's edge. A champion of the honest working classes and the downtrodden, she has yet to ever retreat from a fight she has committed herself to. In addition, Captain Zoë knows a lot about the locations along the rivers of the region; whether it be ruins, caves, camps, or even strange landmarks, she can pass along her knowledge of them to those who have gotten into her good graces.

ZOË TORANNO

Medium humanoid, neutral good

Armor Class 16 (breastplate)
Hit Points 136 (16d8 + 64) 18 16
Speed 30 ft.

STR	DEX	CON	INT	WIS	CHA
18 (+4)	14 (+2)	18 (+4)	11 (+0)	12 (+1)	13 (+1)

Saving Throws Str +8, Con +8
Skills Athletics +8, Intimidation +5, Perception +5, Persuasion +5, Survival +5
Senses passive Perception 15
Languages Common, Orc
Challenge 10 (5,900 XP)

Brave. Zoë has advantage on saving throws against being frightened.

Brute. A melee weapon deals one extra die of its damage when Zoë hits with it (included in the attack).

Sneak Attack (1/turn). Zoë deals an extra 14 (4d6) damage when she hits a target with a weapon attack and has advantage on the attack roll, or when the target is within 5 feet of an ally of theirs that isn't incapacitated, and Zoë doesn't have disadvantage on the attack roll.

Actions

Multiattack. Zoë makes two melee attacks or two ranged attacks.

Maul. Melee Weapon Attack: +8 to hit, reach 5 ft., one target. *Hit:* 14 (3d6+4) bludgeoning damage.

Handaxe. Melee or Ranged Weapon Attack: +8 to hit, reach 5 ft. or range 30/120 ft., one target. *Hit:* 11 (2d6+4) slashing damage.

Drink Up Me Hearties. Zoë can issue a special command or warning to all allied creatures that she can see within 30 feet. For 1 minute, whenever any of those creatures makes an ability check, attack roll, or saving throw, they can add a d6 to their roll provided they can hear and understand Zoë. This effect ends if Zoë is incapacitated.

Appendix A: New NPC Type

MASTER ALCHEMIST

Medium humanoid (any), any alignment

Armor Class 12 (15 with *mage armor*)
Hit Points 99 (18d8 + 18)
Speed 30 ft.

STR	DEX	CON	INT	WIS	CHA
10 (+0)	15 (+2)	12 (+1)	20 (+5)	15 (+2)	16 (+3)

Saving Throws Int +9, Wis +6
Skills Arcana +, Sleight of Hand +
Languages any languages it knew in life
Challenge 12 (8,400 XP)

Alchemical Bandolier. The master alchemist may locate and extract one alchemical substance from its well-organized bandolier of bottles and vials as a free action on each of its turns.

Alchemical Substances. The master alchemist may imbibe or throw an alchemical substance to create a spell-like effect as a Use an Object action. For this purpose, the master alchemist is an 18th level spellcaster. The master alchemist's spellcasting ability is Intelligence (spell save DC 17). Spell-like effects created by alchemical substances do not require concentration, even if their corresponding spell does, and instead last for the maximum possible duration. These substances are completely inert in the hands of anyone but the master alchemist.

The master alchemist has the following substances prepared:
2/day each: *darkness powder* (see **Appendix B: New Items**), *potion of fire giant strength, potion of greater healing, potion of growth, potion of invisibility, potion of speed, smoke powder* (see **Appendix B: New Items**)
1/day each: *dragon breath bomb* (all targets in a 30-foot cone must make a DC 17 Dexterity check, taking 6d6 fire damage on a failed save, or half as much damage on a successful one), *fire bomb* (as *fireball* spell with an 80-foot range), *glue bomb* (fills a 10-foot radius within 80 feet with powerful adhesive for 1 minute, so that a creature in that area must succeed on a DC 18 Dexterity saving throw or be restrained. A restrained may attempt a DC 17 Strength saving throw at the beginning of each of its turns, escaping the area and ceasing to be restrained on a success), *potion of superior healing, sleep gas* (see **Appendix B: New Items**)

Magic Resistance. The master alchemist has advantage on saving throws against spells and other magical effects.

Spellcasting. The master alchemist is a 18th-level spellcaster. Its spellcasting ability is Intelligence (spell save DC 17, +9 to hit with spell attacks). The Master Alchemist has the following Wizard spells prepared:
Cantrips (at will): *acid splash, mage hand, message, poison spray, shocking grasp*
1st level (4 slots): *expeditious retreat, grease, mage armor, thunderwave*
2nd level (4 slots): *acid arrow, gust of wind, misty step*
3rd level (3 slots): *fireball, haste, stinking cloud*
4th level (3 slots): *black tentacles, fabricate, resilient sphere*
5th level (3 slots): *arcane hand, creation, mislead*
6th level (1 slot): *freezing sphere*
7th level (1 slot): *simulacrum*
8th level (1 slot): *mind blank*
9th level (1 slot): *prismatic wall*

Actions

Dagger. *Melee or Ranged Weapon Attack:* +6 to hit, reach 5 ft., or range 20/60 ft., one target. *Hit:* 4 (1d4 + 2) piercing damage.

Appendix B: New Items

ALCHEMICAL SALTS AND PRODUCTS

The so-called "salts" extracted from the strange formations of the Salchamp represent a variety of alchemical substances, many of which have proved valuable in the concoction of the unique substances crafted by Cat's Cradle's alchemists. While alchemicals can duplicate the functions of a range of magical potions, some have effects that differ significantly from their arcane counterparts. Below are listed several of the products whose manufacture is unique to Cat's Cradle, but these represent only a sampling of the many different alchemicals available in that city.

DARKNESS POWDER

Wondrous item, uncommon

When you use an action to toss this powder into the air, it expands to fill a 15-foot radius sphere. The powder absorbs all light, creating an area of total darkness. The darkness lasts for one hour or until it is dispersed by a strong wind. 200 gp/vial

ENHANCED STEEL

Potion, rare

When you spend one minute to apply this salve to a metal weapon or suit of armor, you change its properties. A single treatment causes the item to be magical and to provide a +1 bonus to attack and damage rolls if it is a weapon or a +1 bonus to armor class if it is armor. The effect lasts for 24 hours. Subsequent coatings within the 24-hour period are not cumulative, and subsequent coatings at any time have a chance of ruining the item. Each time after the first that you use this salve to coat a weapon or suit of armor, roll 1d20. If the result is 10 or less, the item is still enchanted, but instead of a +1 bonus, it gives a −1 penalty. 100 gp/treatment

FALSE SCENT

Wondrous item, uncommon

Used by hunters and, less lawfully, by criminals being tracked by dogs or other scent-based creatures, *false scent* comes in small ceramic jars. You can use an action to apply the lotion to a creature, changing its scent to that of a different creature, usually something benign such as a deer or rabbit. A single dose lasts one full day. 50 gp/dose.

INCENSE OF HEALING

Wondrous item, uncommon

One of several different incenses sold in Cat's Cradle and created with Salchamp salts, a stick of *incense of healing* causes all creatures who remain within 20 feet during the minute it takes to fully burn to regain 1d6 + 3 hit points. 150 gp/stick

INCENSE OF SILENCE.

Wondrous item, uncomon

This incense takes 10 minutes to burn completely; during that time, a 20-foot radius is affected as if by a *silence* spell. The effect can only be interrupted if the incense is extinguished. 100 gp/stick

INCENSE OF TRANQUILITY

Wondrous item, rare

A stick of *incense of tranquility* burns over an hour. A creature that rests within 20 feet of it for that time gains the benefits of a long rest. A creature can still only benefit from one long rest per day. 200 gp/stick

SLEEP GAS

Potion, uncommon

You can use an action to throw this item at a location of your choosing you can see within 30 feet. When the glass sphere lands, it breaks and releases a gas that fills a 20-foot-radius sphere surrounding it. Roll 5d8; the total is how many hit points of creatures gas can affect. Creatures are affected in ascending order of their current hit points (ignoring unconscious creatures). Starting with the creature that has the lowest current hit points, each creature affected by the gas falls unconscious for one minute or until the sleeper takes damage, or someone uses an action to shake or slap the sleeper awake. Subtract each creature's hit points from the total before moving on to the creature with the next lowest hit points. A creature's hit points must be equal to or less than the remaining total for that creature to be affected. Undead and creatures immune to being charmed aren't affected by the gas. 100 gp/vial.

SMOKE POWDER

Wondrous item, uncommon

When you use an action to smash this vial of powder on the ground, it expands to fill a 20-foot radius sphere. The sphere spreads around corners, and its area is heavily obscured. It lasts for one hour or until a wind of moderate or greater speed (at least 10 miles per hour) disperses it. 100 gp/vial.

WATER TABLETS

Wondrous item, common

After you use an action to consume a *water tablet* you are immune from the effects of thirst for up to eight hours. Smaller and far more compact than water skins and other containers, *water tablets* are popular with adventurers, especially those who intend to venture into wilderness areas or far from civilization. 1 gp/tablet